Hummingbird

Tristan Hughes was born in northern Ontario and brought up on the Welsh island of Ynys Mon. He is the author of three novels, *Eye Lake*, *Revenant*, and *Send My Cold Bones Home*, as well as a collection of short stories, *The Tower*. He is a winner of the Rhys Davies Short Story Prize and is currently a senior lecturer in Creative Writing at Cardiff University.

Hummingbird

Tristan Hughes

Parthian, Cardigan SA43 1ED
www.parthianbooks.com
First published in 2017
© Tristan Hughes 2017
All Rights Reserved
ISBN 9781910901908
Editor: Richard Davies
Cover design by by RJPHA
Typeset by Elaine Sharples
Printed in EU by Pulsio SARL
Published with the financial support of the Welsh Books Council
British Library Cataloguing in Publication Data
A cataloguing record for this book is available from the British Library.

For my goddaughters, Martha and Rose

Metamorphosis

My name is Zachary Taylor and I mostly grew up in two places. One was a few miles outside a small town called Crooked River in northern Ontario; the other a camp on Sitting Down Lake. To begin with we migrated from the one to the other each season like a small flock of geese; first my mother and father and me, and then just me and my father. We spent our summers at Sitting Down Lake and the rest of the year at the other place, which we never did get around to giving an official name. As the crows flew they were only about forty kilometres apart, but to me they were like two quite separate hemispheres. Back then there was no road linking them, only the railway tracks.

To get to the lake we'd take the train from Crooked River, hitching a ride in the caboose. There weren't any scheduled stops at the lake but, if you arranged things with the driver, he'd bring the train to a swift standstill there, so swift it sometimes seemed it'd not fully stopped at all. I always picture us arriving at a hurried trot, a hobo canter, amidst a frantic tossing of bags and cases. And this is how each summer began – watching the red of the caboose recede into the distance, surrounded by the scattered debris of our stores and belongings as though we were the lone survivors of some kind of disaster.

But once it had disappeared, and we'd turned our heads, a sandy, horseshoe-shaped bay would spread out in front of us, with two small islands of naked rock in its centre and at its mouth three larger ones, topped with pines and spruce and birch. It seems to me now the surface of the lake was always glittering when we arrived. Up close its waters were as clear as air. You could see a long way down. The bottom, even if it was twenty feet below, appeared only just beyond the reach of your fingers. There were big trout out of sight in its deepest parts. If you caught one you could feel the clean cold of that deepness on its body.

For the next weeks, and sometimes months, this would be our home. The real disaster, as I thought back then, was that we ever had to leave it.

Our other home was different. Officially, for the purpose of school and municipal taxes and such things, we lived in Crooked River. But in reality we lived fifteen minutes' drive away; a negligible distance by car but a much longer one in other ways. Crooked River had no suburbs: there was the town, the few homes – like ours – straggled out along the highway, and then an awful lot of nothing for a long way in either direction. You lived in town or you lived out of town, in the bush. Tax purposes aside, there were no purlieus or other in-between places.

Our house sat in a clearing beside a shallow, weed-clogged pool of water which my father called 'the pond' but which my mother – who felt no need to name it otherwise – called 'the swamp'. Its water was tea-bag brown and smelt of rotting leaves and goose shit and slippery dead things. The tamaracks and black spruces surrounding it appeared in constant retreat from its brackish waters, and those which hadn't escaped them stood naked and needle-less in the shallows, as gaunt and pale as pillars of salt.

It wasn't a place to stay put in, and I don't think my parents ever planned to. Like many of their early arrangements in

Crooked River, it was considered temporary. They never did get around to finishing up the house. Its walls were covered in pink siding insulation which over the years faded to grey-white, as though the swamp had leeched out its colour, as it had done to the stranded trees. Out front were the first few planks of an abandoned deck which, if you pinched your buttocks together, you could just about perch on and listen to the cars and trucks whoosh by on the highway. At night their lights seemed to come into the house and touch you. But there were never that many – and every year a few less.

Whether this explains anything I don't know, but my parents began their lives together in Crooked River just as the town itself was passing its climacteric. The iron ore mine had shut several years before; the lumber mill the year after. There were boarded-up windows on Main Street and the only fresh paint in town was on the 'For Sale' signs. Then there was the dust: an ochre-red pall that drifted over from the mine site like the last, wheezy exhalations of a dying lung, settling everywhere on everything. It covered the roads, the rooftops, the leaves of the trees. Even in June it looked like fall.

My mother's hair was the same colour as the dust. She'd been born and raised in Crooked River.

'And I always thought it was the Irish in you,' my father had joked when we first arrived there.

'Well, what do you think?' my mother asked.

'I can live here,' he'd said, looking around at the closed signs and tripping along the rutted street and choking on the dust. She needn't have said anything. He would have lived anywhere she asked him to. He would have lived on Mars, which was almost as red. 'But maybe we could find somewhere that's not *exactly* here.'

And so they'd moved out to the swamp, which my father tried to think of as a pond.

3

He was from the south of the province. He was used to suburbs. He thought it'd be like living in the country.

I was five years old when we moved. At some point I must have heard my parents use the word 'sabbatical'. My father was a junior professor of history at a university in Toronto and had arranged leave for six months, so he could go with my mother to look after her father who had fallen ill. My grandfather owned a dry goods store in town. I remember almost nothing about him as a healthy man. Later, I would discover that in many ways we were similar and I often wished I'd known him in another, in a better, time. But instead, most of my memories are folded together into this single recurring scene: of him lying on a narrow bed in a room above his store, his eyes glittering with an awful brightness, his voice as thin as paper, his pinched, yellow skin as desiccated as the goods he was too ill to sell. The first year my parents stayed they were waiting for him to get better. The next year they were waiting for him to die. And then there were the years after he died, when there wasn't a reason for waiting anymore, except that by then they'd begun to live their lives there, as is often the case with people who think they are only waiting somewhere. I never heard the word sabbatical again.

My father had started teaching history in the town's high school. My mother worked two and a half days a week in the library. When she wasn't working in the library she worked on her hobby, which was carving antlers. Every spring and fall she'd walk for miles through the bush to collect moose and deer sheds. Sometimes, if she was lucky, she'd find an old set of caribou antlers too (they'd vanished from the area fifty years before – for what reason nobody could say). Over the winter and summer she'd whittle them. Mostly she created animals of one sort or another, some of which were recognizable but others chimaeras of her own devising. Many years later, my father would tell me that she'd been taken to an exhibit of Inuit carvings as a girl and these had made a great impression on her. She also liked the Ojibwa pictographs that were hidden away on the cliff-sides of lonely lakes. We'd go to visit them sometimes, and while my father and I ate hotdogs on the shore she'd sit in the canoe and look at them, tracing their shapes on the palm of her hand.

Inside, our house was a strange and fabulous bestiary. In the living room a huge moose rack hung on the wall, with tines that tapered into the heads of fish and otters and an odd creature with the eyes of a lizard and the jaws of a pike. In the bathroom a bear's snout reared out of bone bushes and trees, off of whose branches hung rolls of toilet paper. In my parents' bedroom a set of caribou antlers had been turned into animals with beavers' teeth and eagles' wings and great bulging bellies.

Once, when I was young, I held a set of whitetail antlers on my head and, thinking myself a great wit, said to my mother, 'I'm a deer'. She smiled at me and said, 'You are. And look,' she continued, taking the antlers from me, 'now you're a heron too.' She guided my fingers over them and said, 'See. This is its beak, and here's the curve of its skull.' She told me that in any part of any animal you could find the shape or essence of another. One thing could always change into another thing. Nothing in nature was really as fixed as people thought it was. My father, who was watching us, said the Greeks called this metamorphoses. I didn't know which Greeks he was talking about and when I tried to say the word it came out more like molasses; which at least made a certain sense to me – it was what turned beans and bitter things sweet.

Outside the house my father tried to raise a garden. He

5

bought some tomato plants and watermelon seeds, which he thought was the kind of thing you did when you lived in the country. They sprouted, and then a late frost withered them into tiny yellow leaves. I wondered if this was metamorphoses too.

I was nine years old and my parents and I were happy enough in our little house by the swamp and then my mother sat down one day in the bathtub with her whittling knife and carved her own wrists. She left no note or explanation. The ragged lines on her wrists only said what they said. She was one thing and then she was another thing.

That was towards the end of the winter. A month later the swamp thawed and my father gathered up all of my mother's carvings and threw them, one by one, into its waters. We didn't go to Sitting Down Lake that summer. My father spent most of it sitting in our front room instead. I spent most of it in the reeds and bulrushes that grew around the edges of the swamp. If I looked carefully, and for long enough, I found I could still see some of my mother's carvings through the brown murk of the water. They looked different in this other element. And then the fall and winter came and they looked different again. After freeze-up, but before the first heavy snows came, I'd walk out on the swamp and look at them through the ice. It was only the year after that they began to green over and become invisible. By then I'd begun to realise my father and I were going to be staying put. I think he was waiting again then, but for what I didn't know.

Several years later, afraid I was already forgetting what my mother had truly been like, I dove down into the swamp to try to find her carvings. I recovered only a few. After I'd wiped away the weeds and slime I discovered them once again transformed. These strange beasts, which had once appeared so benign to me, were no longer that. Looking at their taut and twisting tendons, their gaping mouths, their thick- ribbed and bulging bellies, I found myself instinctively flinching from them. There were things there I hadn't seen before and didn't want to see.

But I kept them. And every now and again I still pick them up and look at them and feel their time-worn smoothness in my fingers. I try to imagine they give me access to some part of her beyond my scant and failing memories, some aspect of her inner life I'd been too young to understand. But they remain almost as mute and remote to me as the Inuit hunters who inspired her; there are suggestions, hints and flickers of a departed mind, but beyond these only a mystery – an unnameable animal disappearing into a secret and faraway landscape. In the end we cannot share the true and utter thoughts of others, can never see or feel things as they did. When my mother guided my fingers over the antlers that day and said this is a heron it wasn't a heron I really felt.

Ice Out

When at last we did go back to Sitting Down Lake it was to live. My father couldn't sell the swamp house so we abandoned it. By then they'd put in a logging road which led from the highway to the lake and so now we could drive there and commute into town.

The day we first arrived it was as though I was returning there after the elapse of some great span of time, an era or an epoch or an eon, which in many ways it was: it had been a goodly portion of my short life. I looked out over the glittering bay and the islands and the curve of the horizon and it was as though a glacier had just that second passed over the landscape and scoured it clean. I could barely remember being there before, which was fortunate for me, and I wished it could have been the same for my father. But for him it must have seemed like yesterday.

Our cabin was on the shore of the bay, near the curve of the horseshoe. It was a simple building, made of planks of pine that'd long ago been painted a rusty red. My grandfather had built it, back when my mother wasn't much older than I was. The two of them had shared it in the summers (my grandmother had died giving birth to my mother and my grandfather never did re-marry). The chimney was made of stones he'd gathered himself from the far shore of the lake.

In front of our cabin the lake was sandy-bottomed and shallow, tapering gradually down until, about thirty feet out, it dipped abruptly. Beyond the edge of this drop-off you couldn't see the bottom. I'm sure if I'd ever plumbed its depth in feet and inches, or metres and centimetres, it would have disappointed me. As a child I'd thought it almost infinite. Before our return I'd played a game – I was a good, strong swimmer, and had been since almost before I could walk – which involved lugging a stone out to this drop-off and then diving from it, holding the stone in my hands, seeing how long I could hold my breath and how deep I could get before my ears popped and ached. Never once did I get close to the bottom. I'd played this game for years, and a few weeks after we'd come back I decided to play it again. But this time it was different. As I'd sunk with the rock I'd looked below into the murk and a sudden agitation had taken hold of me, a kind of panic. I can't really say what caused this sensation; I can only say that it felt like an endless plummet into places I couldn't see – as though I were drifting and tumbling like an astronaut cut adrift in space, falling forever into a greater dark. Afterwards, I nursed an unspoken fear of the drop-off and would secretly close my eyes whenever I passed over it, either in a boat or while swimming. And whenever I did this I felt as if I was living my life in reverse somehow: that I was becoming afraid of things I had been fearless of as a child.

I don't recall ever thinking of Sitting Down Lake as a lonely place, although perhaps solitude has shaped my memories and perceptions more than I have realised and others might well have thought it so. We didn't have that many neighbours. On one side of us, about thirty feet away, was Mrs Schneider's cabin, which was pretty much the same as ours but painted blue. Further along the bay, on the other side of the tracks, were the remains of Mrs Molson's house. Then there were Oskar the Finn and Lamar Spiller's places, which were both out of sight; the one beyond a rocky point, the other a few hundred yards up a narrow creek. And that, for several years, was that.

I would have been fifteen years old the year Eva Spiller turned up. I remember how slow the ice was going out that spring. It was still on the lake come the second week of May. In front of our cabin there were rocks and stones spread out all over it in what I'd come to think of as almost a pattern – like one of those ancient circles that cavemen made to welcome solstices, which was just the kind of odd and desperate thinking that tended to occur at the end of a long winter. Every day for weeks I'd thrown these rocks and stones out there to check the strength and thickness of the ice, hoping each time one of them would break through. But none of them had. Some of them were much bigger than the others, from when I'd become especially impatient. I was meant to start my job helping Oskar with his trapping but I couldn't until the lakes and ponds were clear.

And then, late one afternoon, a wind began to blow in from the south; gently at first but growing steadily in strength until by midnight it was rattling our winter windows and bending the jack pines over the outhouse. All through the night I lay in my bed and listened to the lake. It was as though some giant animal had slouched out of the pages of an old book to die there; a kraken or a behemoth; a leviathan. There was a terrible moaning and groaning, followed by the sharp, sudden cracking of gigantic bones. Until, just after dawn, it went quiet and all you could hear – but only if you listened carefully – was a shimmery, tinkling sound, as though a million tiny fairies were playing triangles.

Going outside, I discovered the lake transformed. Huge chunks of ice had been heaped up on the northern shore. There were stretches of open water everywhere; wide channels and jagged circles, almost half of the bay. The rocks and stones had sunk. The remaining ice was melting quickly away at its edges, and this was the tinkling sound I'd heard earlier. My father came out and we stood together by the shore for what was probably only a few minutes but seemed much longer, watching the sunlight glint and dance on the gently riffled, newly released, surface. For six months we had forced ourselves to forget what the open water looked like, how very beautiful it could be.

'Well, well,' my father said eventually. 'Isn't that something?'

To begin with I said nothing. I only looked at the water, which I hadn't seen for so long. I'm not sure what I believed back then (I'm not sure what I believe now) but whenever I thought of what might be beyond death and dying I would think of this light, playing on this water.

'It sure is,' I said.

About a month later Lamar Spiller's boat arrived. Or at least some of it did. The front half arrived on a Monday afternoon; the back half didn't get in until the Wednesday. They came on trucks, which bumped their way down the narrow logging road with their hazard lights flashing and their wide load signs scraping against the new leaves of the poplars. It was a big boat, bigger than anything they used on the lakes around here. They'd had to cut it in half to move it.

Lamar Spiller was rich. He hadn't always been. As a younger man he'd worked as a fishing guide and lived in his father's old summer camp. Over the years he'd probably tied about a million jigs onto a million lines, but one day he'd held one in his hand and had the idea of fixing a small silver propeller onto it. It had worked. Or, more importantly, the fisherman he guided believed it worked (in so many ways fishing tackle, as much as fishing itself, is a parable of faith). Lamar had had the good sense to patent it. He'd called it the

Butterfly Jig and within no time at all he'd made a lot of money. And like many men who come by money late and unexpectedly he'd ended up simply enlarging the dimensions of the life he already had. He added a second floor to his father's old cabin. He got a bigger truck. He bought as many acres around the cabin as he could and named it Butterfly Creek Estate. Always a private man, he surrounded it with no trespassing signs. But they weren't aggressive, as those signs often are. They were more apologetic somehow. Please don't bother me, they seemed to say. I just want to be left alone. And that, for the most part, was how we'd always left him.

But the arrival of the boat was too much to resist. A couple of hundred yards up the tracks there was a culvert surrounded by tall cattails, from where you could see directly into Lamar's yard without being seen yourself. When I went there I found the two halves of the boat sitting on the grass. It looked as if it'd fallen from the sky and split apart, or else been disastrously beached by the swiftly receding waters of a flood, like the Ark on Ararat. But it wasn't an ark, and it wasn't from the bible. Afterwards, I would discover it was a Cape Islander from Peggy's Cove, Nova Scotia.

A few days later I walked down to the culvert after school and found the boat had been put back together. The next morning some men turned up from town and launched it into the creek that ran through Lamar's property – the creek he'd called Butterfly. It was barely wide enough for the boat to fit and was so shallow they only just managed to get it into the water before its keel got good and stuck in the mud and goose shit. It was never going to move an inch after that, which didn't seem to bother Lamar one bit. I could see him standing on the bank, pointing shyly to the men to direct them and nodding his head, smiling and then remembering not to smile. I don't think he'd meant it to actually go anywhere. Why would he? He hardly ever went anywhere himself.

After the men left I watched him climb onto the deck and check through the cabin as though one of them might have tried to stow themselves away in there for some reason. Then he came out and sat on the stern, looking down at the reeds on the banks, some of which were still flat and crumpled from the vanished weight of the snow. From my spot by the culvert it looked as though an insect had landed on his forehead. He had furzy grey eyebrows that were hardly ever still. They started moving whenever he was talking or eating; sometimes they started moving when he was just thinking. Right then he was probably thinking pretty hard about something. They were darting around like dragonflies.

The boat must have appeared odd out there on the creek, I thought, surrounded by the reeds and willows and tamaracks, the forest crowding in on all sides of it; an ocean boat, a long ways from any ocean. Or at least I imagined it must have. I'd only ever seen oceans in drawings and photographs. I'd always pictured them as wide and open and endless and for about a week I went every afternoon to look at Lamar's boat and think about oceans. Sometimes I'd sit and look at it for so long my face would puff up from all the mosquito and black-fly bites and it'd almost disappear behind my swollen cheeks.

The next person I saw on it was a girl. She was perched on the bow, staring as fixedly out before her as a figurehead. She had long, straight black hair and was wearing a white sweater. At first the only thing that appeared to be moving was the smoke coming from the tip of the cigarette she was holding. And then she got up suddenly and kicked the side of the cabin. Then she went around to the other side and gave

13

that a kick too, as though she was angry at the boat for not moving. Then she sat back down on the bow. After a minute or so she lifted her hand up and slowly unfurled her middle finger in my direction. She was looking less and less like a figurehead.

'Jesus H Christ. Haven't you got anything better to do than stare at me?' she shouted.

The cattails by the culvert must have thinned out over the winter.

Wannigans

The next time I saw her I was fishing for pike from the shore of Wannigan Bay. It was the bay along from ours. You could walk to it along the tracks, which looped around the edges of its sickle-shaped shoreline. Most of this shore was sandy and this part of the bay was filled with weed beds and lily pads. On its further side it became rockier, the last curve of the sickle ending in a granite cliff.

It was one of my favourite places. There was something lulling, almost hypnotic, about fishing there. On sunny days like this one I'd fix my eyes on the water until eventually they accustomed themselves to the glittering of the light on the surface and the country below became visible – the stems of the lilies, the silver darting of shiners, the occasional bubbles escaping up from the dark murk of drowned leaf-litter to re-join the air. It was as though, if I waited long enough, the slowed rhythms and movements of this country would become as familiar to me as the one I must stand and breathe in. When I did see a pike I'd often not cast at all, but remain there without moving, watching it, trying somehow to match its stillness with my own. But it never quite worked. There is no way to out-pike a pike. Its stillness is prehistoric: it can wait for eons and eras, while you are stuck with minutes and hours.

'I guess staring really is your thing,' I heard a voice behind me say. It was the girl. She was scrambling down the embankment from the tracks.

15

'I'm fishing,' I said defensively. 'For pike,' I pointlessly added.

'*Sure,*' she said. 'If staring is fishing, then you're fishing.'

I didn't reply. She made her way along the shore and stood beside me. The light winked off the now opaque surface of the water. The other country had vanished.

'Eva,' she said. 'In case you were wondering.'

'I'm Zachary Taylor,' I said. I could feel a crowded, tensing sensation on the right side of my forehead, which I got sometimes when I had to speak to someone I didn't know (which wasn't very often at Sitting Down Lake – or Crooked River for that matter). 'But people mostly call me Zack.'

Eva was wearing a faded blue sweatshirt with the letter Q on it and began plucking at the already frayed edges of the cuffs. Then she started scratching the side of her neck. There was a patch of skin just below her ear that was pink and raw looking, but I was careful not to examine it too closely in case she caught me at it and accused me of staring again. Her hair, I noticed, was brown this time, and shorter, and curly. I supposed she must have had it cut and dyed. Or else I'd not remembered it properly from before

'You want one of these?' she asked, offering me a cigarette from a green box with Export A written on it.

'No, thanks,' I said.

'They call this brand green death,' she said. 'Which is kind of funny, don't you think?'

'Why?'

'You know, because green is supposed to be a healthy colour.'

'I suppose,' I said.

'It'd be like a piece of broccoli killing you. Or being run over by a can of spinach. Or murdered by the Jolly Green Giant.'

16

'I suppose.'

Eva took a long pull on her cigarette and as she exhaled looked around the bay.

'So, what's with the wrecks, Zachary Taylor?'

About fifty yards further down the shore from us were the beached remains of two boats, the last remnants of an abandoned logging camp. Eva started walking towards them and, without thinking, I found myself following her.

'They're called wannigans,' I informed the back of her head.

'What-i-gans?'

I couldn't blame her for asking. When I'd first heard them called that it'd sounded like the name of some goofily lumbering and extinct animal (and indeed the word itself has, to my knowledge, become sadly almost extinct these days).

'Wannigans.'

'What did they use them for?'

'I don't know,' I said. And I didn't, not really. Somebody had once told me they'd used them for hauling the bodies of drowned lumberjacks out of the lake, but I wasn't sure if that was true. It probably wasn't. And besides, ever since I'd discovered my fear of the drop-off I'd consigned it to the list of things I tried not to think too much about.

'They're perfect,' she said, running a hand over the bow of the nearest one.

They were curious enough – with their grey, rotting timbers and collapsed cabins and the intricate bulk of their rusted engines – but I'd never thought of them as perfect before. Mr Haney from Crooked River Museum had come out to look at them once. 'Too dilapidated,' he'd said.

'Even for a museum?' my father had said.

'Even for a museum,' Mr Haney had said.

17

Eva took a Polaroid camera out her back pocket and started taking pictures of them.

'How long have you lived out here?' she asked from behind her camera.

'A few years.'

'What do you think about my crazy uncle's crazy boat?'

'It's pretty big.'

'It's from Nova Scotia. I went there on holiday once. What about you?'

'I've never been there.' My father and I didn't go on holidays. We hadn't been on one since my mother died. 'But I'd like to,' I said. 'I'd like to see the ocean.'

'Some fishermen caught a great white shark in their nets, right off the coast from where we were staying,' Eva said, running her hand along the wood again. 'They brought it back to the jetty and cut out its teeth and hung it up by its tail. When I went to touch its fin its skin scraped my fingers like sandpaper. My dad said, 'Good thing you didn't shake hands with it in the ocean.'

'Are you here on holiday?' I asked.

'God no,' she said, without taking her eye from the camera lens. 'I'm here because they kicked me out of the last place I lived.'

'Oh,' I said. 'I'm sorry.'

'Don't be. I'm used to it. They kicked me out of the last three places I lived. Jesus, they must've been getting desperate to send me here to live with Lamar.'

'Who?'

'The Children's Aid people. They never let me live with him before – even when he asked them to let me. The funny thing is, after next month I'll be old enough to live anywhere I want.'

'Why?'

'Why what?'

'Why wouldn't they let you stay with him?'

'I guess because they thought he was crazy.'

But I'd never thought Lamar was crazy. He was just a quiet, private, rather melancholy, man. There was nothing crazy about that. I lived with one myself.

Eva stopped talking and started blowing on one of the photos she'd taken. 'Look,' she said, passing it to me and going to sit on the remains of the bow. She dangled her feet over the edge and started drumming the old boards energetically with her heels. There were holes in the knees of her jeans.

In the photo the wannigans lay exposed in a bright wash of sunlight. It made them appear oddly buoyant, as though they were hovering a few inches off the sand. It reminded me of something else I'd heard about them: that there'd been two others just like these, and how one night a phantom crew had launched them onto the waters of the lake, never to return. My mother had told me this story. She'd been fond of ghost stories. She'd been fond of the wannigans too and had often brought me here. She'd sit on the sand and look at them while I sat beside her and tried to see beneath the surface of the water.

'That shark,' Eva said, jumping off the bow, 'it must have been swimming right off the beach where we hung out. It must have been doing that every day we were there.'

'I guess it must have,' I said.

She took a couple more photos and then we headed back along the tracks together. 'Are there more things like that around here?' she asked.

'Like what?'

'You know, left behind things – wrecks and ruins and stuff.'

'Sure,' I said. 'Lots.'

'Will you show them to me?'

'Sure,' I said.

'What about tomorrow?'

'I'm working tomorrow,' I told her. 'I've got a weekend job.'

'Doing what?'

'Trapping leeches.'

'Holy shit,' she said. 'That's your job? Seriously?'

'And minnows too sometimes,' I added, as if this made it more serious.

At this point we were passing the remains of Mrs Molson's house. There wasn't much left of it, only a few charred boards and timbers. Beyond it the Burn made its bare and blackened way through the bush.

'And what happened here?' Eva asked, getting out her camera. 'A meteorite? An invasion of leeches?'

A few years before a forest fire had passed a kilometre to the north-east of the lake and, almost as a malicious afterthought – or so it seemed – had reached out a thin, crooked finger and hooked Mrs Molson's house clean out of existence, leaving the rest of us untouched. I remembered watching the smoke on the horizon that day, and my father prowling restlessly around, nervously throwing handfuls of dirt into the air to check the direction of the wind. Three times he went over to persuade Mrs Molson to come and join us on our dock, where we had our canoe ready to escape in. But she was a stubborn woman. 'The wind is from the south,' she kept saying. 'We're safe as houses here.' It was an unfortunate choice of phrase. The fourth time my father went over there was hardly any house left. Mrs Molson was standing beside the tracks, holding an old clock and shaking her head in disbelief. 'But it's from the south,' she'd kept saying, as if the universe would suddenly acknowledge its mistake. But it never did. The thin, crooked finger of the Burn – which terminated almost exactly in the charred remains of her house, as though it were pointing to them – smouldered for days afterwards, reigniting intermittently into little flames. Twenty feet on either side of it the grass hadn't even been singed. The fire hadn't crossed over the tracks at all. Mrs Molson and her clock went to live with a niece in Alberta. We never saw either of them again.

After I'd finished telling her this we turned back and walked as far as the culvert. On one side of it we could see Lamar standing on the deck of his Cape Islander, holding a fishing rod out in front of him as though it were a staff (an unusually assertive gesture for Lamar, making it look as if he were trying to turn back some invisible tide). On the other side of it the treed horizon gently swelled and dipped, like the belly of a giant man asleep and snoring beside a puddle.

'Jesus Christ,' Eva said, looking from me to Lamar and then upwards at the sky, as though she really were asking him. 'Where the fuck am I?'

Swimming

Back at our cabin I found my father sitting hunched over on the kitchen floor, attempting to balance a glob of peanut butter over an elaborate contraption involving a plastic bucket and some kind of tiny ladder. It was his latest version of a humane mousetrap. He could never bring himself to kill them, and each summer would try to perfect some new contrivance for capturing them alive. He was a tall, thin man whose limbs hung as long and awkwardly from his body as Abraham Lincoln's, and as he fiddled over his trap his elbows jutted out at odd and unpredictable angles. He looked like a praying mantis trying to split an atom.

'Did you see Lamar's boat yet?' I asked.

'I saw the front half, on the truck,' he said.

'They put them together,' I said. 'It's sitting in the creek now.'

'Isn't that something,' he said, standing up. His wispy, cow-licked brown hair almost touched the chipboard ceiling. Through the thick, round lenses of his glasses his eyes had the slightly surprised and befuddled expression they habitually had, as though he were a sleepwalker recently woken, in a place he only vaguely remembered.

I hesitated for a moment (there were subjects my father and I were careful not to bring up with each other, or approach too closely) before telling him about meeting Eva.

'Eva,' he said. 'You mean Eva Spiller?'

I nodded.

'You mean Lamar's brother's girl?'

'That's what she said – that Lamar was her uncle.'

My father had moved over to the cupboard and started taking the dishes out of it. He began wiping them clean, one by one, even though they were already clean; a sure sign he was thinking about something he didn't want to think about, and certainly didn't want to talk about. After he'd finished with the plates and started on the cups I left him to it.

Later on in the day, as the sun began to dip into the west, my father and I sat down together on the screened porch and watched Mrs Schneider swimming out towards the two small islands in the centre of the bay. We did this sometimes, although it was never planned or consciously synchronized. We'd just drift into the room at the same time, as though by chance.

Mrs Schneider was halfway to the islands. She wouldn't quite reach them; she never quite reached them; it would have taken an alteration in the dimensions of the world for her to reach them. Every morning and late afternoon she'd set out from the shore in front of her cabin and swim exactly two hundred strokes towards the islands before turning around and swimming the two hundred strokes back to the shore. Her routine had never varied. She was almost seventy-five years old. For Mrs Schneider, to repeat was to persist.

There was something soothing about the invariability of this routine, about the rhythmic splash of her pale arms breaking the surface of the water. It was like watching the sun rise and set over a familiar skyline. And it was during these times that my father would attempt to broach those subjects which we otherwise tried to keep at a safe distance; those subjects which revealed the cruelly ragged and random aspect of the world. He found it extremely difficult to talk about such things but he didn't want me to be ambushed by them either, as we had both been before.

23

'You know what happened to Eva's parents, don't you? You heard about the accident? You remember it?'

I wished then I'd said something earlier and spared him having to ask these questions. Of course I'd heard about it, everyone in Crooked River had heard about it, although my memory of it was far from clear. Fortunately I'd remembered enough not to ask Eva anything awkward earlier. There'd been a family on holiday. There'd been a plane crash. There'd been no survivors. It was a sad and dramatic story and perhaps I would have remembered it more clearly had it belonged to another time. But the fact is it had happened not long after my mother had gone and a peculiar blurriness had overtaken me. It would be difficult to describe this condition, if it was actually a condition at all. (For several months my father's colleagues at the school had tried to convince him to send me for treatment but he'd refused.) I can only say that during this time everything had become obscure and vague to me, not only events and incidents but people and what they said. Everyone around me and their words – the nurse who put her arm around my shoulder, the police officer who drove up our track to ask if my father owned any guns, the girl in school who gave me a lasagne her mother had made for us – all of them, and all they said, had seemed to recede into a distant background. Even if they were standing right there, close enough for me to see their lips moving, they'd seemed like bats in a faraway cave – a darkly twittering chorus whose separate voices I couldn't, and didn't want to, hear.

'I do,' I said. My father was in quiet agonies. You could tell he didn't want to go into the details – they were not happy ones – but felt it was his duty. I could hear one of his knees knocking against the bottom of the table. We both looked out at Mrs Schneider for reassurance. But today something was

24

different. We leaned simultaneously forward in our chairs and craned our necks. It was a multiplication of arms. There was no doubt about it. There were four of them.

'It must be Judith,' my father said.

Judith was Mrs Schneider's daughter and was as rare and elusive a visitor at Sitting Down Lake as a Mountain Bluebird. If she came at all – and some summers she didn't – it was often just for a day or two at most. Sometimes the only sighting we got of her was this one – of the top of her head and her bare arms as she swam with Mrs Schneider. Comparing them with her mother's you would not have thought of them as related at all. One pair of arms was long-boned and fleshy, the other short and wiry; one head of hair was blonde, the other – despite its years – resiliently black. When they stepped out of the water Judith was revealed as at least a foot taller. Standing on the beach they looked like water nymphs from entirely different mythologies.

The reason for the rarity of Judith's visits was apparently her husband, who didn't like it at the lake. I could only recall seeing him once. He'd had a carefully trimmed beard and a bathing suit that was too small for him and bug bites all over his legs. Whenever she'd been near him, Judith had stooped her back and shoulders to appear smaller (he was a good few inches shorter than her, and more slight too). Whatever Mrs Schneider thought of this husband we never knew. Complaining about husbands must have been a very private affair for her, if it was an affair at all. Her own had been dead for nearly twenty-five years, long enough to have become nearly flawless.

We watched the two pairs of arms move out towards the islands, the one seeming to wink and dart through the water, the other to slosh and churn, and then, before reaching them, in a moment of unexpected, and almost perfect, unison, turn

25

and make their way back. And as we watched them it was as though we were gliding silently together past the crashing plane and Eva's dead parents and the cruel, leering face of accident and disaster. My father didn't feel the need to discuss them anymore, which was a great relief to the both of us.

The Leech Gatherer

'Zachary,' I heard my father calling the next morning. He always used my whole name when he was waking me and then, when I was good and awake, he'd switch to the shorter version. He must have thought the extra syllables would help lead me more gently out of my dreams.

It was still dark outside. Through my window I saw several fading stars eclipsed momentarily by the ragged wings of a homebound bat. A paraffin lamp was burning in the kitchen; it cast a soft, faintly liquid light, which gleamed off the lenses of my father's glasses.

'Maybe you should wear an extra sweater,' he said.

The extra sweater was a winter ritual he was slow to relinquish. He'd keep suggesting it until the end of July.

'I've made some Red River Cereal, Zack. You want some?'

This was also a ritual. My mother had tried to get me to eat Red River Cereal. I remembered her asking me every morning if I wanted some, as if eventually I'd simply forget I didn't like it. I guess it was one of her things my father wasn't prepared to give up on; a question of hers he felt still needed asking.

'No, thanks.'

'Are you sure?'

'I don't really care for it,' I said, for probably the thousandth time. My father had a curiously old-fashioned sense of table manners, even for back then. You never 'hated' something – even 'not liking' something was considered a touch strong –

you 'didn't care' for it. As a child I had a rather aloof relationship with various root and green vegetables, as well as the Red River Cereal.

After breakfast, while I stood in the porch waiting to leave, he kept popping his head in and out of the kitchen door and telling me to wait a second. He was trying to remember a line from a poem he'd learnt in school. After about the third time he knocked his glasses off on the door jamb.

'Wait, wait, I'll remember it,' he said, fumbling around on the floor trying to find them. 'It'll come to me any second now.'

He said the poem was all about leeches.

'I've got it,' he announced, appearing extremely pleased with himself and flailing a hand sideways against the coat rail. 'All things that love the sun are out of doors,' he quoted.

It was still dark outside.

The sky began to lighten as I made my way along the edge of the bay, following the trail that led to Oskar the Finn's cabin. It was hardly a trail at all any more. Over the winter the snow and the wind had brought four or five trees down over it. In some places it was no different from the rest of the woods and the only way you could tell it was there was by looking for the gummy scars on the tree trunks where branches had been cut. Fortunately it was hard to lose your way because on one side it hugged the shoreline. At the mouth of the bay the three bigger islands emerged out of the mist and gathering light like the looped back of the Loch Ness monster. There was a big squat boulder on the tip of the headland, which my father called a glacial erratic and everyone else called the Toad, and about three or four hundred yards beyond it was Oskar's place.

Oskar's cabin wasn't like any of the others on Sitting Down

Lake, or anywhere else for that matter. It was like something out of a fairy tale. For a start, it stood on stilts. It was built on a platform constructed around four tree trunks, cut about fifteen feet above the ground so that their tops protruded up from the corners of the roof like extra chimneys. The cabin itself was a higgledy-piggledy affair, tilting a good few inches to the right and made of logs that jutted out at odd and uneven angles. It looked like a building that'd been ripped from its foundations by a passing tornado and, after a spin or two, been deposited in the branches of the forest.

Directly behind it there was a tall white pine and about twenty feet up its trunk, facing back into the woods through ever-watchful sockets, was a bear's skull that had been nailed onto it. There was a second bear's skull above the front door, which you had to clamber up a home-made ladder to get to. This one hadn't been nailed on as tightly and sometimes, when the breeze picked up, would tilt to the left and right as though it were craning on an invisible neck. The air made a slight whistling, whooshing noise passing through it, like the sounds inside a shell – which I'd been told were like the sea.

I'd often pestered my father about these skulls, and why Oskar's place was on stilts.

'It's a Finnish thing,' he'd say, as though this explained everything

I knocked four times and there wasn't any answer. The skull peered silently down at me. There was no wind yet, not a breath of it. I was about to knock a fifth time when the door opened and Oskar shambled past me. It wasn't until he'd gotten to the bottom of the ladder that he appeared to notice I was there.

'You set?' he said.

Oskar often seemed as erratic to me as the boulder. He did what he did and went where he went and saw little need to explain anything. (I was beginning to learn how this was a habit of solitary people.) Except sometimes, even when he wanted to, he couldn't explain what he'd done or how he'd ended up in a place. (I was beginning to learn how this was a habit of people who drank a lot.) During the spring and summer he worked for a man called Jay Boyette, trapping minnows and leeches to sell to the fishermen who used his fly-in camps and outfitting business. I was helping him this year. I'd only been out a few times so far – to get minnows from a nearby pond – but was planning to go with him more regularly when school finished.

Today we were trapping leeches. Down at the dock Oskar started loading the traps into his boat. They were squares of thin aluminium folded into envelopes and tied at the corner with a piece of string.

'Did you see Lamar's boat?' I asked.

He grunted and carried on loading his traps.

'They put the two halves of it back together.'

This time he didn't bother grunting. Apart from Oskar and my father, and occasionally Mrs Schneider, there wasn't anybody to talk to at the lake. Not that any of us were great talkers in any case, but for some reason I felt a strong urge to that morning. And the boat was our big news. I thought about mentioning Eva too but there was the risk it might bring up other subjects, like the accident and her dead parents.

'It's stuck in the creek.'

'Why don't you go get that bait.' If Oskar didn't want to converse there was no point pushing it.

A few yards down the shore from the dock there was a bucket hanging by a piece of old rope from the branch of a cedar, out of the reach of foxes and bears. As I was untying the rope a bunch of bright red blood slopped over the rim

30

onto the front of my jacket. The bucket was full of beef livers.

'That's meant to be for the leeches,' Oskar said as I carried it onto the dock. He was fumbling with his outboard. It didn't have a maker's name; it looked like a mechanical Frankenstein's monster, cobbled together out of engine graveyards. After a few mumbled curses he managed to get it started. The air at the back of the boat smelt of gasoline and bilgy water and Crown Royale whiskey. I went to sit in the bow.

We headed out towards the northern shore of the lake, coming eventually to a long bay shaded by tall pines and poplars which narrowed and tapered until it became a creek full of rocks and snags. I stood up in the bow to direct us. Every twenty feet or so Oskar would stop and put a trap in, stooping over the bucket first to slice up pieces of liver for bait.

'You've got to use fresh stuff,' he said. 'If it's rotten they won't give it a sniff.' I watched him carefully from the bow as he slid pieces of bait into the spaces between the folded aluminium, which is where the leeches would, hopefully, gather. His fingers were shaking, and slippery with the blood.

I never knew exactly how old he was. Seen from a distance you might have mistaken him for a child. He was a short man; barely, if at all, over five feet. He always wore the same red and black check shirt and grey woollen pants, whatever the season or weather, and under the folds of his clothes he was wiry and compact, like jerky wrapped around bone. He must have been over seventy but it was hard to tell sometimes. His features were pressed tight to his face – a flat nose, shallow cheekbones, nothing left exposed. His skin was dark, the rest darker: black eyebrows, black hair, black eyes. He looked native to a different north, a further north.

The creek led into a beaver pond and we manoeuvred

31

around its twiggy edges, setting traps as we went. Oskar spent a lot of time staring into the water as if it were a book he was reading or a riddle he was figuring out.

'Put some shallow and others deeper,' he said. 'You can never be sure where they'll be.'

Because I was concentrating on Oskar and the traps I didn't see it and so wasn't expecting the sound. It was as sharp and percussive as a rifle shot in the morning air and before I'd worked out it was the admonitory slap of a beaver's tail I'd flinched and overbalanced and was under the water. It felt like I'd been punched everywhere on my body at once. Only a while before this water had been ice. I grasped frantically at the side of the boat and tried to haul myself out but Oskar made me swim the extra few yards to the shore. It was safer, he told me.

Once we were both on land he sent me to fetch wood. It was better, he said, for me to keep moving. One thing we learnt in school was that around Crooked River more people died of hypothermia in May and June than in January. People were less afraid of the cold when they saw pictures of trilliums on calendars, and when people were less afraid the world was more dangerous. We didn't have the most optimistic of curriculums.

While I was drying myself out in front of the fire, Oskar started cooking some gobbets of beef liver on the end of a stick, like marshmallows.

'You want some?' he asked. 'It's fresh.'

I said no and began to wish I'd said yes to the Red River Cereal.

By then I could feel my hands and fingers again and decided I'd go fetch more wood. The ground around us was wet and swampy but a bit further back it became drier and firmer. I'd gone about a hundred yards when I stumbled upon the remains of a barrel stove. It was rusted but not all the way through. You could still tell what it had been; I even thought I could see a patch of ash in the back of it – though that might've been dirt. A few feet further on I found the top half of a bucket and the rim of a tin bowl. Behind them was the remnant of a log wall. Three of the logs were still balanced on each other, as though bound there by the moss and lichen that covered them. The rest had fallen and returned to mulch and litter and earth.

It wasn't so unusual to discover abandoned places like this in the bush. It was dotted with trappers' shacks and old logging camps and other places, like our swamp house, that people had simply left behind. It wasn't unusual, but there was something about this one that made me even more shivery in my damp clothes. I hurried back to the fire.

Oskar was finishing another piece of liver. 'What was that place?' I asked, pointing back into the bush. He knew everywhere around Sitting Down Lake, and everything about it. He took his time finishing the liver and then stared at the fire for a while, the same way he'd stared at the water – as though it were a riddle or a book.

'That was the prison,' he said eventually. I waited for an explanation but he offered none.

'What prison?'

'The one for the soldiers,' he said.

'What soldiers?'

'It was a long time ago,' he said. Then he got up and I knew that that was all I was going to get today. We set the rest of the traps and headed back.

I'm not sure whether it was because my clothes were still damp, or that the word prison had conjured certain gloomy associations, but for the entire journey home – and long

33

afterwards too – I found myself uncharacteristically moody and restless, unsettled by a combination of curiosity and misery. I kept recalling details about the place in the bush, details I'd barely noted at the time, and then thinking about them in ways I would have preferred not to.

There'd been two birch trees beyond the fallen wall. Someone had nailed horseshoes onto their trunks and over the years the wood had grown around them so that the iron was all but submerged beneath two large burrs, which were as lumpy and contorted as a witch's chin in a children's book. It seemed awful to me that the original shape of these horseshoes had mutated into something so disfigured and ugly – the very opposite of luck. Long after going to bed their shapes, transformed now into two horridly leering faces, mocked me from the insides of my eyelids.

Eventually, unable to sleep, I got up and went to sit out by the fireplace. My father had lit a fire before going to bed and its remains were still glowing. Earlier, I'd heard the springs of the old chair squeak and groan as he clattered onto it, and then the pages of a book being turned. The embers cast a gentle light over the small table beside the chair. My father had been reading the *Narrative* of the explorer, David Thomson. There was a grey moleskin notebook beside it on the table and picking this up I turned to the most recent of several new quotations copied into it. Thomson was describing a trapper he'd known from York Factory.

'An old acquaintance who had a long range of traps, had neglected to leave firewood at the hut at the end of the range, arriving late in the evening had to cut firewood for the night, with all his caution a twig caught the axe and made the blow descend on his foot, which was cut from the little toe, to near the instep; he felt the blood gushing, but finished cutting the wood required; having put everything in order, he took off his shoe and the two blanket socks, tore up a spare shirt, and bound up the wound, using for salve a piece of tallow; he was six days journey from the factory and alone …'

A long and troubled night stretched out in front of Mr Thomson's acquaintance. I pictured him sitting in front of his fire making desperate and gloomy calculations: what kind of cold would tomorrow bring; what type of ground had to be crossed; how much blood had been lost; how much would he need.

Looking up from the notebook and out of the window, I was surprised to discover a tiny orange light moving slowly along the tracks. It was as if a spark had spiralled up the chimney and managed to make its way there. As I watched, it stopped abruptly and began moving in the opposite direction. After a hundred or so yards it again shifted direction. Back and forth it went, glowing bright and then dim, going out and then, apparently, reigniting. It took me a minute to figure it out: it must have been one of Eva's green deaths; or actually several of them in chain-smoked succession.

From behind his bedroom door, I could hear my father shifting on his mattress. Some part of his anatomy knocked against the headboard, another thudded against the wall. He couldn't sleep (he often couldn't). After stirring the remains of the fire with the poker I sat back in the chair and closed my eyes. It was no use. The leering faces loomed instantly onto the undersides of my eyelids, this time taking on the lurid colours of the embers.

I tried opening my eyes quickly and pretending for a second I'd arrived in this place for the very first time, had stumbled upon it like an explorer. But the fire was still there and the cabin and the orange light moving along the tracks. The whole familiar night was awake with restless and unhappy spirits. And, like Thomson's acquaintance, I would wake up knowing exactly where I'd gone to sleep.

Night Swimming

The next night, determined not to dwell on the prison site, or anything else for that matter, I lay in bed reading one of my grandfather's old collection of *Field and Streams*. They were often a great comfort to me and usually had at least one story about boys fishing for pike, though most of these boys were more concerned with catching them than watching them. I was in the middle of reading such a story when the orange tip of a cigarette passed right by my bedroom window. Whether or not the boy in the story caught his pike, I don't know – I was dressed and outside in about half a minute. The moon hadn't risen yet and it was very dark.

The tip had already reached the Schneider's cabin. I was about to follow it along the path when it veered suddenly away, disappearing behind the cabin where Mrs Schneider had her garden. I picked it up again beyond the rhubarb patch. There were lamps lit in both of the back rooms and I made sure to keep beyond the light that was spilling out from their windows. I didn't want to be suspected of snooping.

I was about twenty feet from the rhubarb when the tip broke into a tiny shower of sparks and disappeared. I stood there without moving. I still hadn't actually seen Eva.

'I can see your problem,' I heard her say. 'It's so much harder to stare at people in the dark.'

I followed her voice until I could just about make out the pale oval of her face through the rhubarb leaves. She was sitting on the ground, holding her knees.

'What are you doing out here?' I whispered.

'I might ask you the same.'

'I followed your cigarette.'

'How sweet of you,' she said. 'Good leech day?'

'Not too bad,' I said.

'Except for the leeches – not so great for them, I'll bet.'

Some moths, headed for the light of the windows, bumped against my head and, startled, I swatted at them as if they were giant mosquitoes. 'Just moths,' I said.

I heard a fish jump somewhere out on the lake.

'That was probably a fish,' I said.

'If you're going to hang about you might as well sit down,' Eva said.

By the time I had she'd already lit another cigarette.

'I don't know what they do to humans but these green deaths sure keep the bugs off,' she said. 'Better than the crap I've been using.' She was covered in mosquito repellent. I'd smelt it the moment I'd opened our front door and up close the smell was so strong it was almost choking me. She must have used a whole bottle of the stuff. All around us in the dark insects must have been dying.

From where we were sitting we could see right into the two back rooms of Mrs Schneider's cabin. In one of them, Judith was sitting stooped at a desk sorting through a pile of what appeared to be letters and papers. In the other, Mrs Schneider was sitting in a chair, knitting, surrounded on all sides by colossal piles of junk.

'What's with all that?' Eva asked admiringly.

'Oh, that's just Mrs Schneider's room.'

'That bit I kind of guessed.'

'It's where she puts her stuff.'

I didn't really know how to explain it otherwise.

Another of Mrs Schneider's daily routines was her walk along the tracks. She'd take it a half hour before noon, alternating the direction she went in each time, and during the course of these walks she'd pick up anything she found and carry it back with her. It was endlessly surprising what you could find near the railroad. People seemed to throw the oddest things out the windows of the trains. And invariably these objects would find their way into Mrs Schneider's back room, a room she appeared to keep solely for the purpose of storing them and which bore very little, indeed no, relation to the rest of her cabin, or indeed her life.

While the rest of her existence was meticulous, everything in this room had been thrown pell-mell in random heaps and piles. It was a chaotic mess – the only space kept open being the one for her chair. Over the years, through secret glances and glimpses (obviously, she didn't show anybody the room) I'd watched these heaps and piles grow. I'd seen umbrellas, shoes, innumerable hats; including an actual top hat – a relic from when the circus trains had passed by this way. I'd seen books, magazines, paper lanterns; the arm from a tailor's dummy; a pair of red silk gloves; a wax couple from the top of a cake. The list could go on.

I could never work out, and never would, the reason for this hoarding; as far as I know it was Mrs Schneider's version of Dorian Gray's portrait. It was one of the things about the lake my mother had told me and my father when we'd first come here, explaining how it was something we shouldn't bring up. In fact, we rarely mentioned it among ourselves, except if we lost something when we were at the lake. 'I guess that's for Mrs Schneider's room,' we'd say.

'Wow, just look at all that shit!' Eva said, swaying her head from side to side in appreciation. 'Is that a rocking horse?'

Inside the other room, Judith was still sorting through the papers and letters. It was her old bedroom and there was a large brown trunk on the bed. Occasionally she'd lean over from where she was sitting at her desk, pluck some more papers and letters out of it, and add them to the ones on the desk. There were already too many. The desk – an oddly miniature thing, no doubt left over from her childhood – had been almost overwhelmed by them. A large pile, covering most of its surface, swayed and tottered. Stray sheets kept falling off its sides onto the floor. Underneath it, in a sort of mirror image of this excess, Judith's legs were cramped into a space far too confined for them. Everything in this room appeared too small for her.

Whether it was because of this confinement and clutter, or because of the content of what she was reading, it was evident that Judith was becoming gradually more irritated. She began knocking individual papers onto the floor. She brought her fist down onto the pile. And then, suddenly, she stood up, knocking the whole desk over. After a second or two, she picked up a handful of the fallen papers and letters and, standing back up, started tearing them up one by one. I liked seeing this version of her – not slouched or stooped but at her full height: shoulders back, chest thrust defiantly forward, as if in rebellion against the puny world.

Next door, Mrs Schneider continued with her knitting.

'Jesus, someone's pissed at something.'

'That's Judith,' I said proudly.

As we made our way out of the rhubarb patch and back towards the path, Eva asked me if I wanted to go swimming.

'But it's dark,' I said.

'You've never swum at night?'

'But I don't have a bathing suit.'

'That's what I like about you, Zachary Taylor – you're so spontaneous! Don't you live next door?'

'I'm not sure what the water's like?'

'Wet, I imagine. Anyway, suit yourself.'

She turned and began walking up towards the tracks. For a while I remained standing where I was. I could hear the lake slopping quietly onto the sand. The truth was it wasn't the time or the temperature of the water that bothered me; it wasn't even the question of bathing suits. What bothered me was the darkness of the water. It was what had come to frighten me about the drop-off; only at night it was as though the drop-off had spread its dominion everywhere. Up at the tracks I saw the flare of a match and then the glowing tip of a cigarette.

By the time I'd caught up with her, Eva had reached the culvert. She told me to wait there for a minute and slipped off towards Lamar's place. From beneath my feet came the sound of the creek slowly sluicing into the lake. Somewhere a muskrat slipped out of the reeds and into the water. A hang-nail moon had risen over the horizon.

'Let's go to the place with the old boats,' Eva said when she got back. I could just about make out a small bag or bundle in her hand.

'You mean the wannigans?'

'The whatever-i-gans.'

When we reached them, she disappeared into the remains of one of their cabins. After a few minutes she re-emerged slowly, snaking out a pale leg followed by a pale arm; and then a weirdly frilled and sack-shaped body; and, finally, an unnaturally white head, as smooth and hairless as a salamander. Under the frail light of the half-nail moon it looked as though some underground creature, which had

41

evolved pink-eyed and beyond the reach of the sun, were groping its way out of a cave.

'Ta-da!' she said, jumping down onto the sand and holding up her arms like a chorus girl. 'What do you think?'

She was wearing a white swimming cap and a swimsuit that must have come from several eras before. The top half was made up of the elaborate folds and bunches of an ancient blouse, while the bottom half became a shapeless knee-length skirt that might have appeared racy to my grandmother and which I assumed had probably once belonged to hers.

'At least you won't get cold,' I said.

We walked along the beach until we'd reached the rocky edge of the bay. Beside us the cliff loomed above the water, its inky mass blocking off a portion of the night sky, its shape stencilled in an absence of stars.

Abruptly, without saying anything, Eva turned, took a handful of splashing steps, and plunged into the lake. It took a second or two for my eyes to find her in it. She was turning in somersaults, parts of her becoming briefly, flickeringly visible above the dark surface of the water – a pale leg, an arm, the smooth white dome of her head.

I stripped down to my boxer shorts and waded in. Or rather I took one step in, enough to wet my ankles. I couldn't take another. I felt dizzy and breathlessness, gripped by a kind of vertigo, as though I was on the edge of some incredibly high precipice. For a while Eva continued to turn in somersaults. Then her head popped out of the water a few feet out in front of me, like an albino seal, or a talking egg.

'Can you swim?' it said.

'Of course I can!'

'Are you afraid of water?'

'No. Well, not like that.'

42

'Like how then?'

It was very complicated, I told her.

'Yes,' she said. She was close enough now that I could see she was stroking her head. 'It sounds *very* complicated.'

Frustrated and exasperated I tried to explain.

'It's more like the dark water. When I think about it, it's like I'm standing on the edge of somewhere really high. And I'm about to fall. And it's like there'll be no bottom and I'll end up like an astronaut adrift out in space.'

'*So* complicated. And *so* poetic.'

I wished I hadn't said anything then and the things I wanted to say I couldn't; my mouth felt like it was stuffed full of dry crackers. I wished I could take another step into the water, close enough to kick her.

'Hold on. Wait here a second,' she said as she stood up suddenly and began sloshing her way over towards the edge of the beach. I watched her pale limbs and head disappear into the dark. After a few seconds the sounds of sloshing were gone and I could hear the rustle of branches and the snapping of twigs. And then for a while I couldn't hear anything.

'You mean like this?' she called out eventually.

Her voice was coming from above me. She was standing on the top of the cliff. You could just about make out her outline.

'Hey, be careful,' I said.

I wasn't sure how deep the water was beneath the cliff. And I knew she didn't know.

'Point made,' I called up to her.

'Like an astronaut, you say.'

For an instant, her outline seemed to become more defined, to almost glimmer, as though the sliver of moon had got brighter. And then it was gone. It was a long way down.

43

When it came, it was more a wet thunk than a splash.

'Eva,' I called out.

The air was cooler than I'd realised and my bare skin had begun to break out in goose-bumps. The soft hair on my arms and legs was sticking up. I took a step. Somewhere ahead of me I knew there was a drop-off. Closing my eyes I took a second step.

'Eva?'

An image came to me, one that had often been part of my dreams when I was younger but which hadn't returned to me for a long time. I was standing on the bottom of the lake, surrounded by drowned lumberjacks. They seemed to be importuning me but I couldn't work out what it was they were trying to say or what they wanted. Their features were blurred and exaggerated by the water; their noses too long, their lips fat and swollen, their eyes unnaturally large, as though swelled and bloated. Above me, in a pale blue circle of light – which could have been the sky – I could see the faces of the men in the wannigans. They were reaching down towards me with long hooks.

'Eva?' I called out, more frantically this time, dreading the third step.

Opening my eyes, I found the white oval of her head bobbing in front of me. She was smiling.

'You could have hit the rocks at the bottom.'

'I could have,' she said. 'And I didn't.'

'You could easily have hit them,' I said, feeling suddenly exhausted.

'And I didn't.'

She'd stood up and started walking out of the water. When she got to the shore she walked right past me, heading quickly up the beach towards the tracks.

'Be seeing you,' she called back.

44

I'd been about to follow her but instead I stood where I was, shivering, up to my shins in the water, wearing my underwear, thinking about drowned lumberjacks and drop-offs and phantom boat crews, my heart beating too fast for all the wrong reasons.

Highway Kids

There was still a week of school left. The next day was a Monday and I was surprised to find Eva waiting for the school bus at the end of the logging road, where it joined the highway. My father dropped me off beside the stop sign. Even though he taught at the school he insisted on me catching the bus there instead of driving in with him. I guess he thought it'd help me make friends with people my own age which, now that we were living out at the lake, he must have considered important (although in this regard it was hardly different from the swamp house).

'Good Morning, Zachary Taylor,' Eva said, stubbing one of her green deaths out on the tarmac. Her hair was definitely blonde. It was in a different style too, pulled back into a long ponytail. She was wearing a red and green plaid dress, like a girl in some kind of private school brochure.

'Most people say Zack,' I said.

'Really. Most people.' She looked around theatrically in several different directions.

'Hello,' she shouted. 'Hello there, most people.' Her voice echoed off the rock-cut that ran along the other side of the highway. 'I prefer Zachary,' she said.

Down in the ditches at the sides of the road the cotton grass was showing white against the new reeds and shoots of grass. Here and there on the verges you could make out the orange and yellow dots of early hawkweed flowers. The summer had already arrived. Around here there was barely time for spring.

'Why are you going to school?' I asked.

'What the fuck else is my uncle going to do with me?' she said, smiling. 'How's the leech business?'

But before I had a chance to answer the bus came wheezing around the bend. Our stop was as far it went. Beyond Sitting Down Lake you had to figure out your own education.

My father might well have reconsidered the bus as a way of me making friends if he'd actually ridden on it. I'd once overheard one of my teachers telling a newly arrived colleague about us. She called us highway kids. 'They can be difficult sometimes,' she'd warned. 'They tend to be … a little less socialised,' she'd said, searching for the right way to put it. And, in all honestly, we were a motley crew; a curious ragtag of schisms and sects and me. There were two Mennonite boys, with pale hair and pale eyes, who wore matching white shirts and black pants. There was a boy called Freddie, who was a few years younger than me and lived at the end of a dirt track in a maze of old boats and chicken houses. His parents were Seventh Day Adventists. Then there were three blonde sisters, the Betchermans, who lived a long ways out in the woods and belonged to a family who were so religious people said it wasn't even a regular religion they followed – that their parents had kind of made their own up. In which case, they'd done a fine job. Amongst themselves, the sisters were perpetually cheerful and laughing and as sleekly fit and active as seals. As opposed to Freddie, who was taciturn and blotchy and every morning looked as though he'd just discovered a stone in his shoe. The two Mennonite boys never spoke at all. The Betcherman sisters aside, our pilgrimage to school was usually a study in silent contemplation.

Eva plonked herself down on the seat beside Freddie and started talking to him. At first he looked astonished. Then he

47

looked nervous. Then he looked happy. Then he couldn't shut up. It was quite the transformation.

Within about ten minutes she knew more about him than I ever had. She asked him what a Seventh Day Adventist was. Freddie, sounding more scholarly (sounding more anything) than I'd ever heard him be at school, told her about William Miller and how he'd predicted Jesus would come back to earth on October 22nd 1844.

'And did he?'

'Not in the way they were expecting.'

'What did they do then?'

'They called it The Great Disappointment.'

'I guess it must have been.'

I didn't hear the rest of their conversation. We were five kilometres out of town and even though the track had grown over and there was nothing to be seen from the highway anymore but trees and water and rock, I knew exactly the spot we were passing, just as I knew every single time I passed by it. Eva and Freddie's lips were still moving, but I couldn't hear them anymore. Each time I passed the swamp house it was though someone had pressed the mute button on the world.

Then I could hear them again. Freddie was telling Eva how his family had their Sunday on Saturday. We'd gone by the town population sign (which nobody had bothered changing for many years) and the bus was bumping over the tracks and past the old rail trucks and bunkhouses and abandoned machinery. A haze of reddish dust from the mine still hung over Crooked River, especially after breezy days, although sometimes it was hard to distinguish it from rust. Most people in town had two vehicles: one to drive and one to turn slowly orange in the front yard. Your first breath in town usually tasted slightly ferric on the tongue.

As we pulled into the entrance to the school I heard Eva asking Freddie where the town offices were. I leant over my seat and asked what she needed there.

'I need a map,' she said, smiling. I was beginning to realise that Eva's smiles were no indication at all of whether she was pleased or happy or not.

'Why do you need a map?'

She smiled.

She was smiling when we got out at the school. She was still smiling as she lit a green death and walked right back out of the entrance. She stopped to take a picture of the broken pinball machines sitting in the car park outside of Burky's Pool Hall and then disappeared around the corner.

Freddie hovered for an extra second or two in front of the doors to watch her before, reluctantly, obeying the call of the bell and returning to the long silence of his school day. Disappointment came in all sorts of different shapes and sizes.

Maps and Exploration

I should have told Eva that if it was a map she was looking for then she was heading in the wrong direction.

Our school was covered in maps. It was as though the geography classroom had gone wild and annexed the entire building. They'd been painted onto the sides of the corridors and made into murals on the walls; they hung in picture frames above our lockers; whenever I looked up I was surprised not to find them on the ceiling. There were maps of the town site and maps of the surrounding country; maps of the way taken by European explorers; maps of the old voyageur routes and the railroad; maps of the survey lines that had made sure we weren't in Manitoba or Minnesota. I could think of several reasons for this: that Crooked River was incredibly proud to have found its way onto a map; that places obsessed by maps are places that are afraid of falling off maps. But the main reason – the one I tried not to think about – was my father.

In the months and years after my mother died my father had become absorbed in a very specific history: that of the European exploration and settlement of the area we lived in, as well as the land to the north and west of it. It wasn't the history in which he'd specialised at university (his thesis had been on 19th century Canadian economic history; he'd stayed in the boardroom, so to speak, rather than setting out in the canoe) or one, as far as I knew, he'd taken an undue interest in before. All I really knew was that at some point after she was gone the living room of the swamp house had become cluttered with accounts by Verendrye and Hearne and Mackenzie and Thomson. He'd read them all through the day and the evening. And when I woke up in the morning I'd often find him still sitting there in his chair, as if he'd stared all night at the place on the page where the dark had overtaken him, waiting for it to get light enough for him to see the words again – the words of all those restless men, brought to a halt in the hands of one who for weeks and weeks hardly moved an inch. These days, whenever I step into a museum, or happen to glimpse one of their names on a street sign, I picture their accounts teetering in the stagnant murk of that room, what light there was tinged a mossy green by the swamp. There they loom still, like the ivied columns of long-abandoned temples, hidden in jungles where even the birds are silent.

For a long time I couldn't figure out what it was he was looking for in those accounts, only that the results of his looking were writ large on the walls of the school. He'd begun to teach a course on exploration and early settlement and each year his class would paint a map on the walls to illustrate what they'd learnt. And written alongside these maps were selected quotations from the explorers and travellers. These were chosen exclusively by my father (they were usually selected from the passages he copied into his grey moleskin notebook) and I'm not sure if anyone else on the faculty had ever bothered to read them that carefully. If they had, they wouldn't have found the usual commemoration and celebration of civic beginnings and accomplishments. It was as though my father had trawled each account in search of its lowest ebbs, the moments of greatest hardship and despair. The walls of our school told a

51

salutary tale about the dangers of hope and discovery: a careful reading of them would have suggested that if you were to leave your front doorstep you'd most probably freeze to death, or starve, or drown, or worse.

To escape them I got into the habit of avoiding school whenever I justifiably could – during free periods, at recess, any time it was possible. Mostly, I just wandered around town. There weren't that many places to go, not if you wanted tarmac or snowploughs to make the way easier for you. Sometimes I'd follow the river to the old railway bridge or head west towards the remains of the mine site; sometimes I'd go east and make it as far as the abandoned farm. But a lot of the time I'd simply follow the streets until they came to an abrupt end at the tracks or the edge of the bush.

At the end of one of these streets there used to be a motel called the Red Rock Inn. Back then there'd often be men with red-veined, leathery faces, who wore baseball caps and suspenders for their pants, sitting on the cement steps outside, waiting for the bar to open. Usually, they'd be smoking and whistling songs about the Big Rock Candy Mountain or the Sunny Side of the Street. In those days it seemed like everyone over about sixty only ever sang songs from the depression. I guess bad times, like the devil, had had all the best tunes.

The Red Rock Inn had a stripper on Wednesdays and Fridays and Saturdays. There'd be a different one every week; they travelled from small town to small town like salesmen and performed three times a day, once during the day and twice at night. Their names were put up in black letters on a yellow sign outside. Miss DVS. Miss Hunter Hayes. Miss Nude Saskatoon. One day – it must have been a Wednesday – instead of the men, I found a woman sitting out on the steps smoking a cigarette. She was wearing a pink plastic coat that came down to her knees.

'Hey there,' she said. (I must have been looking at her.)

'Hey,' I said.

'Shouldn't you be in school?'

'I've got a free period.'

'Aren't you the lucky one. My name's Chloe. Why don't you sit down,' she said, patting the step beside her. Chloe must have been her real name because it wasn't the same as the one on the sign. Normally at this point I would have begun to feel the tensing sensation in the right side of my forehead and tried to leave, but there was something warm and safe and kind about her and it didn't even start. Up close I could see her face was covered in a powder which reflected the yellow of the sign, making it look soft and golden, like pollen on water.

Chloe asked me some questions, about school and what my hobbies were and things like that. We'd been sitting there for maybe ten minutes when she got up and said she had to go back in. I realised suddenly I didn't want her to go. I'm not sure what I was thinking, but I found myself asking her if she wanted to come out to our house and visit. I said I'd like her to meet my father; that they had a lot in common and so they'd probably get on pretty great (I'd not actually asked her anything about herself). There was a pleading, desperate tone in my voice.

'Oh honey,' she said. 'That's sort of sweet but I think maybe you've got the wrong idea here. That's not what I do.'

'But my father's lonely,' I said.

'I'm sorry to hear that,' she said. 'I really am. But I've been to a hundred of these towns and in my experience a lot of people in them are lonely.'

'But it's not his fault,' I said, and then it all came out; about the reading of the accounts and the sitting in the chair all day and the quotations on the school wall. And then I couldn't stop myself and I was gabbing about the antlers in the swamp and how he'd thrown them in there and that sometimes he'd go stare into the water where he'd thrown them for hours and hours and that there were days when I was too scared to leave him alone, even for a second, even though sometimes I didn't want to be around him at all. I just kept telling her things. I didn't know what'd come over me. I wasn't used to talking to people at all, let alone ones I didn't know.

'Oh honey,' she said, reaching over and pulling my head into the space between her shoulder and her neck. I hadn't realised how hot and red my face had become and the plastic of her coat felt wonderfully cool and smooth. 'I'm so sorry. I won't lie, I'm not a hundred per cent sure what it is you're telling me about, but I'll tell you this in return: you've got to try to forget some of that stuff or it'll eat you up. Listen, sometimes I close my eyes and then open them real fast and try to imagine it's the first time I've been in this world; that it's as new to me as it was for Adam and Eve. And if I can do that just for a second, just for half a second, then I know everything will be okay.'

It was only then I began to realise how every time my father started a new account by one of his explorers that was exactly what he was hoping to do; that that was exactly where he wanted to get to. But he never ended up there. He ended up in the place on the walls instead.

Chloe had to go back to work but before she went she said, 'You should try, honey. Promise me you'll at least try.'

'I will,' I said.

And for months afterwards I thought about her and what she'd said. I wanted to do what she'd told me. I wanted nothing more than to feel my cheek against the coolness and smoothness of that plastic coat forever. There were lots of things I didn't want to remember but I was so young there weren't enough years to hide them away in yet.

Un-named Water Bodies

'These "Un-named Water Bodies",' Eva said, scratching at the red patch on her neck, behind her ear. She didn't seem to be in the best of moods. She wasn't smiling and the patch was at least a millimetre or two bigger than before. You could see it clearly below the line of her bobbed hair, which today was a strawberry blonde. 'What's the deal with them?'

'They probably did have names once,' I said.

'So why aren't they on this frigging map?'

'I guess they never got around to asking what they were.'

The map Eva had got from the town offices was spread out on a pinewood table. Reading it you could see how the invention of the settlers had been first taxed, and then exhausted, by the sheer number of lakes and rivers and creeks they'd found here. In a better history they would have listened more carefully and used the names they'd been given by the people who already lived here. Sometimes they had, but often they hadn't. And so they'd gone through their usual repertoire – Loon Lake, Jackfish Lake, Trout Lake, White River, Rushing River, Rainy River – until in the end any old name would do: Big Lake; Less Big Lake; Little Lake; Next River; Next-to-Next River. And then, beyond even these, were the 'Un-named Water Bodies'.

'So where are we then, exactly?'

I tried pointing out the spot on the map but the truth was I was distracted by everything else around it. We were in Lamar's place. I'd never been inside it before. I'd never really expected I would be.

Lamar had about ten no trespassing signs on his land and as far as I knew had never had a single trespasser. Sometimes I'd catch him stalking the edges of his property, waving his fist at some surprised dragonfly or squirrel. He was practising at being a testy curmudgeon, a role – the wildlife aside – he was far too reserved and gentle for. The recluse part he was much better at.

I'd thought his eyebrows were going to jump off his face when Eva had shown me in the door. He had a long nose that seemed to pull the bottom half of his face downwards at the same time as the top half danced this way and that. He nodded at me and I nodded back.

'You never said…' he'd mumbled in Eva's direction.

'Jesus, Lamar,' Eva snapped. 'It's a human being. He won't bite or dirty the carpets, I promise.'

He nodded again, as though he'd decided this was the least risky way of communicating all around, and then slunk back into the corner of the room.

It was certainly a big enough room for slinking. It had a high ceiling and a balcony running along one side, with doors leading off it into the rooms on the second floor. Most of the surfaces were the same shiny, almost glowing, orangey wood; the sign of a more expensive class of pine panelling. One wall looked as though it'd got in the way of a stampede. There were three moose heads peering out of it, as well as a couple of bears and five Whitetail bucks. The opposite wall was covered in fish; Walleye, Pike, Bass and Lake Trout. There wasn't a species in there you couldn't have caught or hunted within a mile or two of the front door. Lamar didn't travel. Or so I'd always thought.

In between the fish and the animals was a wall hung with framed photographs. A quick glance revealed that most of them included what was quite clearly a young Eva, together

57

with a man and a woman who I assumed were her parents; a fact confirmed by the presence in several of them of Lamar himself, who was easily recognisably as the man's brother. As far as I could tell they were mostly holiday snaps. In one of them Eva and her parents were standing at the side of a road beside a blue Oldsmobile, pointing towards a sign I couldn't quite make out. There was a lighthouse in the background, sat on an outcrop of bare, smooth rock. In another, Lamar and his brother were on the deck of a boat holding fishing rods. A third showed them standing beside a shark, clutching the same rods and grinning, pretending they'd caught it. Eva was sitting on her father's shoulders. She was holding onto his neck with one hand; with the other she was reaching out towards the shark.

'So where exactly is Sunset County Outposts,' she demanded. 'In relation to here.'

Sunset County Outposts was what Jay Boyette called his fly-in fishing and hunting camps. His hangar and float planes were based out at a lake called Windigoostigan, about five kilometres to the east of us. Eva looked at the spot on the map I'd pointed to and then, quickly and gently, brushed it with her fingertips. Lamar appeared to have moved a few feet closer to us. The two battling halves of his face had settled into a kind of grimace, an uneasy armistice between alarm and resignation.

'God, stop lurking will you,' Eva suddenly said. 'I hate it when you lurk.'

'I'm sorry...' Lamar replied. There was a pause, a subtle skip of breath, where an endearment would have been. You could tell he wanted to use one but didn't know which one to use, or if it'd be okay to use it. The easy, relaxed version of him I'd seen in the photographs hadn't looked this awkward with his niece. I wondered how many times he'd actually seen her since then.

'Let's go to my room,' Eva said.

While most of Lamar's cabin was full of dead animals, Eva's room was full of dead places. Its walls were plastered with hundreds of Polaroid pictures, each one a study in abandonment and dereliction. There were decaying fishermen's shacks from the Maritimes and half a wall of old barns from the south of the province and the prairies, their boards as weathered and grey as elephant skin. There was an outdoor ice rink with poplar saplings growing out of its centre, and a rusty gas pump on the side of a road whose crumbling tarmac was tufted with grass. In one corner I glimpsed the wannigans, in another the mine site at Crooked River. Eva was a collector of ruins.

She was also a collector of other things. Through the half open doors of a dresser I could see a line of white, Styrofoam heads, each one topped with a different wig. I recognised the blonde ponytail from the school bus and the curly brown one from Wannigan Bay and the straight black one from when I'd first seen her. There appeared to be others too but the doors weren't open wide enough for me to make them out. To begin with I was surprised but, of course, how else had her hair always been changing. And besides, once I'd had a second to think about it, it didn't seem such a bad or strange thing at all: to be able to change a part of yourself and have a place where you could keep all the different versions. Wasn't that just metamorphosis?

At first I thought it wise to keep my mouth shut. I didn't mention the dresser and tried my best not to look too obviously at the walls. Eva had rolled her map out on the floor and was marking circles on it with a red felt-tip pen. She pressed so hard in one spot the tip went through the paper. The outline of the old railway bridge in town edged its way into the corner of my eye. A rickety fire tower seemed to fall right into my line of sight. It was hard not to look. It was hard not to ask. I picked the easier question.

59

'Why do you take pictures of stuff like this?'

'Because I like to,' Eva replied testily. 'Why do you trap leeches?'

I could see a pile of mouldering logs beside a creek. Some ancient-looking stumps. A few pieces of rusty wire leaning twisted around the remains of a plank.

'Holy crap,' I exclaimed, as if I was her.

She glanced up from her map.

'Where'd you take that?' I asked, pointing to the photo.

'Just outside of town. Why? What's so special about it?'

'It's the farm.'

'What farm? It didn't look like a farm to me.'

I doubt it would have looked like a farm to anyone. I doubt it had ever once looked like even a *possible* farm to anyone; except, briefly and long ago, my great-grandfather – when he paid a token price for its hundred acres and dragged his young wife and son up north to join him on it. It's a difficult task examining and accessing the decisions of your ancestors – after all, the sum total and result of those decisions is you – but the fact is my own had something of a knack for making poor ones.

So while all the other new arrivals in Crooked River had tried to find gold or iron or jobs with the railroad and logging crews, my grandfather's family had tried to start a farm. I can't imagine what they were thinking. There was a good reason those other settlers had pinned their brightest hopes on what lay under the earth rather than on what they could raise out of it. There *was* no earth, not to speak of. The glaciers, like a bad tempered army in retreat, had scoured the most of it away. It wasn't farming country. This was Abel's land. And if you'd listened carefully it was the blood from Cain's scraped and weary knuckles you'd most likely have heard crying from the ground.

60

How they must have come to curse it, that one hundred acres. They held on there for almost exactly one calendar year. My grandfather, if he spoke of it at all, described it month by month, as if reciting some drear and doleful almanac.

They arrived in May, with the ice just off the lakes and piles of snow still sitting in the shady places. They waited for it to melt and the land to dry. June came and almost went. And still they waited. And still it didn't dry. My great-grandfather came into the tent one day with a handful of bulrushes and tears in his eyes. Half the land was a swamp. The black flies, who knew better, arrived there to breed. My grandfather said their faces swelled up so big and red and round it was as if children had drawn them with crayons.

The other half of the land was granite and spruce and sand and moss. The whiskey jacks got fat on the grass seed that wouldn't grow. The slugs ate the green beans. At night they could hear muskrats slipping into the creek.

In July an eagle took the first of the chickens. Not knowing what might thrive best in this place they'd hedged their bets and brought a few of everything. There were two milking cows, three goats and four pigs. There were sixteen chickens and half a dozen geese. There was a black and white collie and a ginger tomcat.

In August a fox took the rest of the chickens. The tomcat got into a fight with a lynx and lost. In the small patch of land my great-grandfather had cleared and burned over, the grass lost the swiftest of battles to the mullein and thistles and fireweed. The cows lowed disconsolately in their makeshift canvas barn. Their milk had stopped. In desperation they'd started munching on Labrador Tea. The mosquitoes wreaked a quiet and itchy havoc on their udders.

September saw two of the pigs light out for the territories. They may or may not have been the smart ones. The other two contracted strange fevers from rooting through the swamp. The log cabin they were trying to build kept slanting alarmingly to the left and there were so many gaps in the walls it didn't need windows. One of the goats got crushed by a falling tree.

On the tenth day of October a wolf ate the collie. And then, seeing as there wasn't anything left to watch and herd them, the rest of the goats.

In November the geese decided to join their wild brethren and flew south. Nobody had got around to clipping their wings. They were definitely the smart ones. It started snowing the day after Halloween that year.

Three days before Christmas one of the cows froze to death.

He never even mentioned January and February and March. They were like those suspicious blanks and elisions in my father's explorers' accounts: empty spaces haunted by unspeakable things.

On the fourth day of April the second cow slipped through a thin shelf of remnant ice at the edge of the creek and drowned. The creek was only four feet deep, but the poor creature was so thin and starved it seemed to just lie down. She'd given up, my grandfather told me. She'd had enough. And a month later the rest of them had too.

Before leaving my great-grandfather pulled all the nails out of his ramshackle cabin and useless fences and sold them. For the first time in a year he actually made some money. It was better than farming. Around here anything was better than farming. The dry goods store opened within the year.

'Jesus,' Eva said after I'd told her all this as best I could. 'I guess they were pretty unlucky.'

'That's exactly what they would have said,' I told her. Whenever my grandfather talked to me about the farm he'd always said how unlucky they'd been. But how unlucky is it if an eagle eats a chicken? Isn't that, given the circumstances, in all probability quite likely to happen? I'd never been able to figure out if thinking you were unlucky led you to make bad decisions, or if it was the other way around. Why people chose to do what they did. It was something I'd thought about a lot – and spent a lot of time trying not to think about too.

'Why do you want to know where Sunset County Outposts is?'

Eva scratched her neck for a second or two. Then she looked carefully at the photographs on the walls, as if the answer were in one of them somewhere.

'You know what happened to my parents, don't you? It seems like everyone else around here does.'

I told her that's what Crooked River was like. I told her I'd heard some things but I didn't really know – not all the details. There was a picture of a derelict motel behind her. 'Live bait and ice' it said in cracked paint on a sign outside. I kept my eyes focussed on this.

I couldn't quite hold Eva's gaze, which was concentrated and intense and angry.

'Well, I want to know.'

'Know what?'

'I want to know where,' Eva said, brandishing the map at me. The pen had gone through in a few places now. Tiny pinpricks of light were shining through the holes. 'I want to know exactly fucking where.'

The day before, as we'd checked the leech traps, I'd asked Oskar about the accident. I didn't much want to hear about it but had asked anyway, thinking that now Eva was around it was something I should probably know more about. Oskar had seemed unusually glad to talk to me about it (I knew he was leery of the area in which it had happened and tried to avoid it if possible). He'd kept adding details whenever I'd strayed onto other subjects, like the prison for instance.

In any case, this is what he'd told me. The plane in which Eva's parents had died had gone down somewhere north of Sitting Down Lake. It hadn't, according to those who knew about such things, been a straightforward crash. They'd found pieces of the wreckage scattered over an area of about fourteen or fifteen square kilometres. Apparently, the pilot had attempted an emergency landing on a small lake and, when this first attempt failed, had taken the plane back up and begun to circle in search of another place to land. It was then, for reasons no one could be one hundred per cent sure about, that it had exploded in mid-air. They'd found the propeller and the nose and the floats. They'd found the remains of the pilot. They'd even found some of the Spillers' luggage. What they'd never found were the bodies of Mr and Mrs Spiller. There were three small lakes in the area, as well as numerous swamps and ponds and creeks. They'd searched the area for two weeks. They couldn't dredge all of it, Oskar told me. They couldn't search for ever.

I didn't tell Eva I knew any of this.

'Will you help me look?' she asked. Her voice had become gentle now. 'Could you get me somewhere near there?'

'Near where?'

'There,' she said, pointing to the small blue patch that represented one of the un-named water bodies. 'I think it was there.' There was a hole from the pen tip right in the middle of the blue.

I didn't know why she thought it was there, or why she'd want to go there, but I said I would if I could. I wanted to help her, and I wanted to please her too. But secretly I was thinking I didn't really know if I could or not. There were no roads anywhere near it. And in the bush things looked a lot different than they did on a map.

'Okay?' she said.

'Okay,' I said.

And then without a word she walked over to the dresser, reached inside, and took out the brown curly wig.

'Turn around,' she said.

The next thing I knew, she was standing beside me wearing it. We sat down together on the floor, resting our backs against her bed. For fifteen minutes or so we just sat there, not saying anything. Now and again I'd steal a glance at her face expecting, because she'd mentioned her parents, to see something there. After my mother died I'd thought for a long time that I'd been physically marked or altered by it in some way. I'd thought there was a transparency in grief: that it made you horribly visible, like a body turned inside-out. I hadn't learnt then how it was the opposite that was true.

'What happened to your Mom?' Eva suddenly asked.

'She got sick.'

'I'm sorry.'

'There's no need to be,' I said. 'It was a long time ago. She was just unlucky.'

Pictographs

Lamar was out near the creek when I left. He was standing with his back to me, in front of a large pile of lumber which had been delivered the day before. A spare, lean man, he appeared frail before it and much older than his fifty or so years. There was something indescribably sad about the way the fabric of his pants crumpled around his thin buttocks.

I was trying to slip past him towards the culvert, in order to avoid the awkwardness of a meeting, when he turned abruptly around. His half-grin of dismay must have been exactly mirrored by my own. We no longer had Eva as a mediating presence, and were too close to each other not to say anything.

Lamar wasn't an easy man to talk to. My father sometimes joked that he needed some version of talk with a much smaller denomination than just small. At the edge of adulthood I'd worked out my default conversation pieces for most of the situations I found myself in Crooked River. They were seasonal:

The ice was late/early going out this spring.

The snow was going to be early/late this fall.

The real winter cold was coming/here.

It was a bad summer for bugs.

'The bugs are pretty bad this year,' I said.

'They are,' he said.

He swatted several from his forehead, as if to further confirm this. We stood there. I began to edge my body around with tiny steps so I'd be facing towards the culvert; to turn fully around and start walking towards it would have required another sentence. Lamar was rubbing the knuckle of one thumb with the other thumb so hard you could see it beginning to redden.

'I like your boat,' I suddenly blurted.

His face stilled; his eyes relaxed and brightened. He stopped rubbing his knuckle.

'It's an ocean boat,' he said.

We both turned to look at it.

'Have you ever been to the ocean?' he asked me.

I didn't answer for a long time. It was so unexpected. I'm not sure Lamar had ever asked me a question before.

'No,' I said. 'But I'd like to.'

'It's quite the thing.'

We continued to look at the boat. We were in unprecedented conversational territory – and had already come to the end of it. Lamar turned and gestured to the lumber as though it was waiting for him. I nodded towards the culvert and started walking.

I wished I'd had another answer. The closest I'd got to an ocean had been a journey we'd made when I was eight along the northern shore of Lake Superior. We'd gone to look at some Ojibwa pictographs that my mother had seen more than a decade before and was keen to revisit. It was a long drive and it was already dark when we arrived at our campsite.

The next morning, before anybody else was awake, I crawled out the door of my tent and slipped through a fringe of pines. On the other side of it a long, sandy beach spread out far to my right and left. For a moment I stood transfixed on the sand. The exhilaration of the wide horizon, of the open, sunlit space over the water: it was exactly the feeling you would have got from first seeing the ocean. Afterwards I ran as far as I could along the firm, damp sand at the water's edge.

I could have stayed on this beach all day but my mother was eager for us to set out so we could get to the pictographs. But the closer we got the more this eagerness appeared to morph into a kind of anxiety; it was almost as if she feared that, after all this time, they might have been rubbed or eroded from the rock. She spoke about the first time she'd been there. She'd spoken about this trip the day before, as we'd been driving, and much of what she said now was only a repetition of the same details – how she'd travelled there with two college room-mates; how they'd stopped to swim in a nearby river; how the car had broken down and the great adventure they'd had getting back – except that the warmth of the previous day's nostalgia had been leached out of them. There was a hollow, coldly ritual sound to what she said now, like the recitation of a liturgy no longer quite believed in.

When we arrived she set off quickly down the trail towards the lake, my father and I following behind. The trail was rough and stony and eventually descended into a steep, sheer-sided ravine. The light barely reached us down there. It was gloomy and damp, with slabs of wet stone for steps. Above us was a huge boulder that had fallen into the ravine and, after a few feet, had become wedged between its walls. And though it must have been there for centuries, it appeared worryingly recent and precarious, threatening at any moment to continue its fall and block our exit. Keeping our footing on the slippery rock must have been difficult, and our progress slow, but my overriding impression is of my mother's hair bobbing reassuringly out in front, leading us through this place like a flame.

It was a relief to reach the lake. The sun was shining on the pale granite cliffs, which were lapped by water that was a soft turquoise in the light before it dropped off and away into a deeper, darker blue. To reach the pictographs you had to make your way along the cliffs by way of a narrow, downward-slanting ledge. Beyond the cliffs you could see a headland jutting out and some wooded islands sat out from the shore. Several heavy ropes had been attached to the edge of the ledge and dangled into the lake below, for mooring boats I supposed.

My mother was still in front and began to make her way along this ledge, with me close behind and my father coming last. Twice he managed to slip on the smooth surface of the granite and ended up manoeuvring himself on his hands and feet like some gigantic and prehistoric insect. The ropes, I realised, weren't there for boats but in case anybody fell into the lake below (which didn't seem to perturb me; as I've mentioned before, I was less afraid back then).

The pictographs were painted a rusty red, similar to the dust of Crooked River. Like my mother's sculptures, some were quite naturalistic while others were more strange and fabulous. I recognised a caribou, a bear, and some men in a canoe, but it wasn't until glancing at the information sign as we returned to the trail that several sinuous, flowing shapes were revealed to me as a turtle and a heron.

There was one creature that had looked to me like a Stegosaurus with the head of a buffalo. 'That's Mishipeshu,' my father had said, pointing to a drawing of it on the same sign and reading the explanation written below. '…the great water lynx…'

'Please, can you stop,' my mother said as she came up behind us. My parents had exchanged places for the trip back and she was lagging some way behind us, her anxiety replaced by an uncharacteristic listlessness. She'd been silent the whole while we'd looked at the pictographs.

'Stop what?'

'Can you stop reading that sign,' she'd said, as if exhausted. 'Just let them be what he wants them to be.'

As we were leaving the parking lot and rejoining the highway my father took one hand off the steering wheel and wrapped a long arm around my mother's shoulders. As the car gathered speed their whispers came at me in bits and pieces before they were swallowed up in the whoosh of air through the windows.

'But aren't they the same as before?' I'd heard my father ask.

'But that's the problem! They are the same. Don't you understand that?'

I'd switched my attention to what I could see receding through the back window: the wooded islands off the shore, the wide, empty horizon; the high, open sky above the glittering water; the headland, the pale cliffs, the darker rocks at their base.

Now, as I recalled these scenes, I found myself adding certain details from Lamar's photographs to the landscape – placing a lighthouse on that headland, some seaweed on the rocks, scattering some buoys to bob in the swell. I thought if I could do this, if I could reshape this memory, then in fact it would be as though we had been to the ocean. We *had* gone there on holiday. What you could change and alter could never be finished or complete or dead. This is what I had been told back then, and what I had tried very hard to believe in since.

Yes, that is what I should have replied to Lamar's question. I should have told him yes, I had been. I actually stopped at the culvert and turned back for a second as though it might be possible to change my answer. But the moment was gone. He was already picking out boards from the pile of lumber and spreading them on the grass. What was he building? I should have asked him that, I thought. He'd asked me a question. It hadn't occurred to me I could have asked him one in return.

Homesteaders

After over a week Judith Schneider was still next door. Every extra day she'd stayed we'd begun to suspect it could only mean a calamity of some sort or another. Whenever my father saw her out the window he'd involuntarily start cleaning whatever cup or plate was closest to hand.

One afternoon Mrs Schneider arrived at our door, knocked on it vigorously, and announced that she and Judith were cooking homesteaders that evening. Homesteaders were deep-fried jam sandwiches, which I supposed had had their origins in her early, pioneering days. (She'd first arrived here from Austria as a seventeen-year-old girl, having emigrated in response to an advertisement searching for wives for men who lived in the north. She never once mentioned what her life had been like back there, to make her take such a risk.) Homesteaders were also social events, one of the few that Mrs Schneider allowed to interrupt her daily routine. She didn't play cards or drink alcohol.

'Of course, Zachary and I would be delighted to join you,' my father said, having to bow his head slightly to get it below the door frame. Mrs Schneider nodded her own head, which was her version of a smile. She had always approved of my father's manners.

I watched as she made her way back along the path with precise and tidy footsteps. There was something truly impressive in her seeming imperviousness to wear and tear and time – the hair that wouldn't turn grey, the skin that hardly ever appeared to wrinkle, and never tanned. As she reached the edge of her garden I saw her spot a fallen pinecone, adroitly side-step it, stop, turn, and then stoop effortlessly down to pick it up and put it in her pocket. The wilderness held no dominion over Mrs Schneider's property.

'She studies winter,' Mrs Schneider announced, as though she were not quite fully assured this was a fitting subject for professional inquiry.

My father had asked Judith what kind of thing she studied. We knew she worked as a wildlife biologist but not much beyond that.

'I wouldn't say winter, exactly,' Judith said. 'But I do work on winter habitats; specifically, the one under the snow. It actually has a name.'

Judith seemed to fill one side of the room, my father the other, as though the both of them had eaten the cake that made Alice big in Wonderland. She was constantly trying to reposition herself in a way that made her body appear smaller. She slouched and stooped and squeezed. My father blinked and fidgeted. Between them was a wooden dresser, on top of which sat a plate illustrated with a picture of an Alp, and beside it a framed photograph of Mr Schneider. Both of them were in constant danger from my father's long, bony hands. Every time he spoke, he flailed them nervously in their direction.

There was a long pause.

'What is it?' he asked.

'What's what?'

'The name. You mentioned it had a name.'

'Oh that, yes. Of course. The Pukak. They call it the Pukak. It's an Inuit word.'

'The Pukak,' my father repeated.

73

'It's an entirely different world,' Judith said. 'Most people don't even suspect it's there.'

'Isn't that something? The Pukak.' My father repeated the word in a soft, marvelling voice, while knocking his elbow against the dresser.

'You see,' Mrs Schneider added, moving our attention towards the table where the homesteaders were sitting, 'like I said – winter.' She pushed a plateful towards us. She was at an age when eating was extremely important, much more so than what you did or studied.

'But it's only one habitat…' Judith began.

Mrs Schneider – who'd clearly had enough of winter – interrupted her. 'Judith's husband has gone.'

'He's not *gone* anywhere, mother,' Judith protested. 'We're separated. We're getting a divorce.' She looked at my father and I as though what she was saying was in a foreign language that only we understood.

'Like I said, he's gone.'

I'm not sure Mrs Schneider recognised the concept of divorce. Proper husbands were considerate enough to die. The photograph of Mr Schneider looked obligingly down from the dresser. He was tall and quiet-looking; his heart attacks concealed beneath a thin, fragile smile.

'He's not *physically* gone anywhere, Mother.'

My father began gallantly to shovel homesteaders into his mouth. 'This blueberry jam, Mrs Schneider,' he spluttered through the crumbs (breaking one of his own cardinal points of eating etiquette) 'is excellent.'

'Last year was a good year.'

He nodded in my direction, signalling to me to pick up my pace. I already had one in my mouth so pushed an extra one into my cheek. They were remarkably dense and took longer to chew than you would've thought. The homesteaders had

74

been hardy people. My jaws ground to a halt after a few seconds.

'We'll have to watch Zachary here or he'll finish them all off.' My father gave me an oddly contorted look, admonishing me with one side of his face while encouraging me to speed up with the other.

'Ah, but let him Mr Taylor. They have such a sweet tooth at his age. But out here it's a treat for them.'

Judith, looking resigned and relieved, reached over and picked up three.

By the end of the evening I was so full I could barely move. As my father went to leave, he narrowly avoided toppling Mr Schneider. Judith, coming up behind him, knocked her father with her elbow and sent him sprawling to the floor. The plate and the Alp survived.

Outside it was getting dark. There were fireflies in the bushes along the lakefront and bats flickering above the trees.

'The Pukak,' my father said as we walked back along the path. 'Isn't that something?'

Despite the gathering darkness I could see he was smiling to himself, which really was something.

Nature Sleeps

I went to sleep thinking happily of winter but was lifted abruptly out of it by the whistle of a passing train and deposited into a stifling tangle of sheets and blankets. It had been one of those days when the heat of the sun seems to hide away in the cracks and shadows and come out again in the night. I was drenched in sweat and lay in my bed for a while trying to imagine what it would be like to live under the snow. But it was no use. It was too hot and humid.

Outside was no better. The sound of frogs and crickets filled the air like hot breath. Whatever moon there'd been had sunk behind the clouds and it was so dark and still it was difficult to distinguish the water of the lake from the sky. The whistle of the train sounded once more, from what seemed an impossible distance. Beneath invisible trees the fireflies flickered in the undergrowth like explosions on a midnight battlefield seen from some great height.

I shuffled my way to the tracks and began walking along them in search of a breeze. But there was none and I'd not got very far before the dark began to feel just as thick and oppressive as the air. And then I heard a movement of leaves ahead of me, no more than a gentle flickering – the kind a breeze would have made, if there'd been one. I stopped. My mind was suddenly clear and empty and queasily aware. About ten feet in front of me there was a crunch on the chippings. And then another.

'Eva,' I whispered. I thought she might be out wandering.

The next crunch was even closer. I could just about make out something in front of me. It was something far more indefinite than a shape: a kind of visible movement, dark slipping through dark.

'It's me,' I whispered croakily.

There wasn't any reply. I didn't think it was Eva any more.

In the fast beating of my blood I began to think of all the wild things I knew; of the bears and the wolves and the wolverines; and then of the ones I'd only imagined: the sasquatches and the windigos and the little people of the forest. My mother had been right. Nothing in nature was fixed. It was forever half-sculpted. Why shouldn't it contain spirits and beings and monsters; creatures of older worlds; creatures of worlds that hadn't yet been or become?

'It's me,' I repeated. My voice felt as small and weak and wavering as a candle flame.

But by now the figure had begun to take on more definite dimensions and forms. They were reassuringly small. It was Oskar. He was almost directly abreast of me. I could just about make out his face. He was looking from side to side but when his eyes passed over me there was no hint of recognition, or even any acknowledgement I was there. We were only a foot apart.

'Sisko,' he mumbled as he walked past.

And I knew to keep quiet.

Oskar was looking for his sister. It happened sometimes – always at night – and had done ever since I'd been coming to the lake. The first time I'd encountered him like this I'd been with my parents. There'd been a full moon and the three of us had walked up to tracks so we could get a better view of it reflected in the lake.

'Doesn't everything look different,' my mother (who loved such nights) had said.

77

It did. The silvery light had altered the most familiar shapes and features. The islands in the bay seemed, un-anchored from the day, to float back and forth across the mouth of the bay. Trees and branches had been spread and twisted into new canopies. Even the season seemed confused and uncertain, as if a covering of frost had slipped out of winter and found its way into the warm summer's night.

We were close to Mrs Molson's house – which was still standing back then, its white paint glimmering coldly and solidly like marble – when we saw a small figure emerge from the shadows at its side like some elf or dwarf sneaking out of a midnight kitchen.

'It's Oskar,' I'd said.

'Good evening,' my father called out to him. 'What a beautiful night!'

My mother had instantly shushed both me and my bemused father.

'Leave him be,' she'd whispered. 'He's looking.'

'For what?' my father had asked.

She'd put her finger to her lips.

Later, when we were back in the cabin, she told us that when Oskar had been a child he'd had a sister. They'd lived with their parents – who'd emigrated from Finland – in the section house (this was before Mrs Molson had lived in it). Oskar's father had been the section man. A section man was somebody who was allocated a certain section of the railway to watch over and maintain. For many years, Oskar's father had assiduously tended to the stretch that looped around Sitting Down Lake – a fact which somehow made what happened worse. How exactly it had happened nobody knew, even my grandfather hadn't been certain, but the sister had been hit and killed by a train. What was known was that it was Oskar who'd found her. Afterwards, the parents moved away to another section of the railroad, taking him with them. But later, in fact almost as soon as he was old enough and able to, he'd returned.

Whether he was sleepwalking, or in some kind of reverie, or just very drunk, I don't know, but after these episodes you'd often find him lying unconscious in random places around the lake, though never more than a few hundred yards from the tracks. At various times I'd found him in one of the wannigans, behind the Toad, and in Mrs Schneider's garden. My mother had referred to these as his 'nature sleeps'. She'd told us not to wake him. And if he happened to wake as we were passing we were not to ask any questions. How far he walked during these nights, I never knew.

Once the sound of his footsteps on the chippings had receded I knelt down and pressed my ear against one of the tracks. It gave no relief to my skin. Not even this steel was cool. The train had passed some time ago but I still kept listening, hoping to catch some faint after-hum or tremor in the metal, some phantom reverberation.

It was my mother who'd taught me to do this. Her one great fear while we were at the lake had been that I'd be hit by a train. Perhaps it had been inspired by the story of Oskar's unfortunate sister. It wasn't an entirely unfounded or irrational fear – the bends and rock cuts around the lake could conceal a train until the last second; the wind could easily carry away the sound of its engine and whistle – but it was, unusually for her, an exaggerated or disproportionate one. From early on, she'd impressed on me a sense of the tracks (a sense it took many years for me to dispel) as a dangerous and unpredictable place, a kind of grim conduit along which destruction and accident might abruptly intrude into the safety of our summers. As a precaution, she'd shown me how you could pick up the signs of an approaching train from miles away if you pressed your ear against the smoothed metal of the track and waited for the faint, tell-tale vibrations.

How clearly I remember her first showing me this: the way she knelt on the chippings; the faded blue of her jeans; the tiny scar on the back of her neck, almost invisible against the white of her skin; the cascade of her hair falling over the silver of the track and the black of the cinders and seeming to give its colour to the iron ore pellets that had spilt from the rail trucks; the brows knotted in concentration; the way her lip lifted slightly to the right when she smiled at me; the long, soothing fingers; the freckles on the skin on the back of her hands. How clear it all is. And how opaque and inexplicable: this fear that the great disaster of our lives would come from far away, stalking unheard through the bush on ribbons of steel, when all along it must have been lurking there right beside me; something taking form unseen, even as we listened, in a crooked maze of synapses; the warmth of their small and myriad explosions something I could have reached out and almost touched and perhaps even felt.

Prisoners

'What did they do there?' I asked.

They were meant to be working lumber, Oskar told me. But they spent a lot of the time just playing cards, especially when it got cold. 'Regular cards too – you know, rummy and crib, that sort of thing,' he added, as though still surprised that Germans would be able to play them. He told me they sometimes asked him to join them in a game when he happened to be passing by. They must have craved new faces. And except for him nobody passed by.

'There were two guards meant to be looking out for them but sometimes there was just the one,' he said. 'The other would go into town on a spree. Or sometimes both of them would. This was guard enough.' He nodded, indicating everything around us.

A gust of wind shuffled and bent the new reeds at the edges of the beaver pond. Their greenness, so feverishly bright when the sun was shining, had been dulled by the thunderheads above. The sky was big and wide enough to watch the storm circling around the horizon just a mile or two to the west of us. Most people would have landed and started looking for shelter but Oskar didn't appear overly concerned. He was unusually garrulous. Maybe it was the storm. More likely it was the leeches. We'd done well so far. The amount we had in the totes must have been making him giddy. He'd already been drunk when we started out. I'd discovered him beside his woodpile and waited an hour for him to wake from his nature sleep.

The place I'd found before had been a prisoner of war camp. Oskar told me there'd been about thirty German prisoners there. It'd been in operation for about two years.

'It didn't look like a prison to me,' I said, gesturing towards the bush. The truth is I didn't want it to have been a prison. I pictured barbed wire and watchtowers and searchlights; men with gaunt faces walking slowly around a perimeter; trees with no leaves; somewhere a dog snarling and barking. I didn't want this forest, which I was slowly learning to love, to have been a prison. Couldn't anything be just what it was?

'It looked like a regular lumber camp,' Oskar said. 'That's what it was before. That's what it was after. And that's what it was mostly like when they were in it too.'

'But it was still a prison,' I said despondently.

'I guess so,' Oskar said.

'What did they look like?'

'I'll tell you, they didn't all look like the supermen the papers made them out to be like back then. They looked like regular guys.'

I was glad to hear it. I wanted them to look regular. The more regular they looked the less they would have been like prisoners.

'Except they had these big red circles sewn onto the backs of their jackets and shirts,' Oskar continued. 'They used to joke about it. "How can we escape with these targets on our backs?" they'd say.'

A flash of lightning lit up the lopsided tops of the white pines on the horizon. The far side of the pond burst into noisy droplets. A squall had sheared off from the main body of the storm and been flung carelessly in our direction, like the arm of a man turning over in troubled sleep. I wished we could land. I was beginning to feel like I had a target on my back. Oskar carried on checking and repositioning the traps. The leeches in the totes undulated like sunken black flags on miniature pirate ships, merging together now and then into thick, dark, sinuous tangles which were almost the size of my fist. The leeches were a great mystery to me.

'Why change spots when we got so many in these?' I asked anxiously. It was difficult to throw my voice over the seething din of rain. It was falling all around us now.

'They move,' Oskar shouted. 'They change places when the water changes.'

It had been raining when I'd first got up that morning. It'd drummed on the roof and dripped from the gutters. After offering me Red River Cereal and suggesting an extra sweater my father had quoted another line he'd remembered from the poem. 'And all the air is filled with the pleasant noise of waters.' Once again, he'd appeared extremely pleased with himself for remembering it. I'd hoped he'd stay that way all day. Being pleased or happy had for many years been a precarious condition for him; it often presaged him toppling into an opposite one.

'How far from here did that plane go down?' I suddenly shouted. I hadn't planned on asking but out it came anyway. I hadn't promised Eva Spiller I'd help her but it felt like I had.

There was no need to say which one. Oskar squinted at me through the rain. I expected him to say nothing. I'd already been pestering him about the prison.

'Not so far,' he said finally.

'Can you get near it from here?'

He shrugged his shoulders. 'If you wanted to,' he said. I could barely hear him. I could tell he'd had enough. I tried one last question. I'd been meaning to ask it before.

'Did any of them escape?'

'Who?'

'The prisoners.'

He ran his hand over the back of his neck and stared down into the liver bucket. The edge of the storm was passing over us now. The wind picked up and up until it was turning over the leaves of the balsam poplars, exposing their brown undersides, making it look as though the storm had huffed and puffed the forest into fall. Oskar was yelling something at me.

'Let's get the rest of these leeches and get out of here,' he was yelling.

The storm had already passed by the time we got back. In our cabin I discovered all the knives and forks and spoons spread out on one side of the kitchen table. They were worryingly bright and glittering. They must have been polished so hard the metal had got hot. I wanted to tell my father about the prison but at first I couldn't find him. I checked the shed and the woodpile. I knocked on the outhouse door. I walked up to where he parked the truck. The truck was there but he wasn't and I began to feel it then: the slow familiar creep of anxiety, settling on my skin like a sweater made from prickly spiders' feet. Eventually I ran out to the end of the dock, where I could get a fuller view of the bay. It was from there I spotted him. He was sitting out on the point, in the dripping shade of the Toad.

I went back inside. On the other side of the table were a pile of books and his moleskin notebook. I flicked quickly through it. I occasionally checked it like this when he wasn't around, hoping to find something different. I thought maybe, after the night of the homesteaders and his smile as we'd walked back and him remembering the line from the poem, it might be. I flicked through to the latest entry. This time he'd chosen another excerpt from David Thomson's *Narrative*. Thomson and his two guides had capsized on the Black River and lost most of their equipment.

'Late in the evening we made a fire and warmed ourselves. It was now our destitute condition stared us in the face, a long journey through a barren country, without provisions, or the means of obtaining any, almost naked, and suffering from the weather, all before us was very dark...'

The Burn

I was showing Eva the Burn when we spotted Lamar driving an Oldsmobile along the logging road towards Butterfly Creek Estate.

'Oh, God!' she said.

'What's the matter?'

'You wouldn't understand,' she said.

'Understand what? It's just a car.'

'It's just too fucking weird is what it is.'

At the time I was thinking that about almost everything except the car. Eva was pretty weird. At home was weird. It was weird for me being in the Burn. I'd only walked through it a couple of times before. It was like the drop-off: if I could pretend it wasn't there then I did.

At first Eva had been disappointed the remains of the house were gone. But she'd brightened up as we'd walked further on.

We'd followed the path of the burn for about half a kilometre, moving slowly between the charred tree trunks, until we reached a shallow valley formed by two burnt-over hills. They'd been stripped nearly naked by the fire and were curiously dome-shaped, with the skeletons of trees here and there on their summits. They looked like black minarets topped with charred crosses. Eva had wanted to climb one and check out the view. She was a redhead today and was wearing a flowing, smock-like white dress, the kind people used to get baptised in. She must have stood out for miles, like the snow-shoe hares that turned colour before the snow came.

As we'd walked up the hill she'd started picking up burnt pine cones and cradling them in a fold of her dress as though she were gathering fallen plums. I told her how the heat of the fire made them open and release their seeds. And how the ash fertilised the ground they fell on. It was the kind of thing I sometimes thought about to make myself feel better about the burn, whose random destruction otherwise depressed me. I guess this knowledge was a consolation of sorts for me, but Eva had seemed happy enough without it.

'And this is what it left behind,' she'd said. I'd assumed she meant the fire. 'I wish I'd brought my camera,' she'd said and then started darting from trunk to blackened trunk as though we were playing hide and seek. I'd never seen her so playful, so frolicsome; a flickering white spirit in all this desolation.

From the top of the hill you could trace the burn against the green of the spared land and mark the course the fire had taken, veering in loops and ox-bows and meanders – in the dark, charcoaled travesty of a river. In the other direction was the horseshoe of the bay and the thin blue ribbon of Butterfly Creek. It was from up here I'd spotted Lamar arriving in the Oldsmobile. Even from this distance you could tell it wasn't new. He must have bought it second-hand from someone in town. I'd seen Eva's mood change the instant she'd set eyes on it.

'Too fucking weird,' she repeated.

As I watched Lamar parking the car she threw one of the pinecones at me. It wasn't exactly a playful throw. The fire had baked them as hard as rocks.

'Quit it,' I said, feeling the side of my head. 'That hurt.'

She threw another. This one hit me on the shoulder.

'What's wrong with you?' I said.

'You wouldn't understand,' she said again huffily.

Sometimes when she said I didn't understand something it was a statement, other times it was a provocation or an act of frustration. It was hard to figure out which was which.

'But I *don't* understand,' I said.

'Didn't you notice anything when you were in the cabin?'

I hadn't, apart from the obvious things. 'He's got a lot of moose heads,' I said.

'No shit, Sherlock. Did you even *look* at his pictures?'

Partly to give me time to remember and partly to change her mood and avoid another pinecone, I tried to change the subject and told Eva about finding the prison. I thought maybe she'd be interested in photographing it. It seemed to work.

'What direction is it in?' she asked. 'Can you see it from up here?'

I pointed north. 'No,' I said distractedly. 'It's in the bush. You have to be right there to see it.'

I was trying hard to remember the wall of pictures in the main room of Lamar's cabin. I hadn't noticed anything especially unusual about them then and I couldn't think of anything now – except maybe how similar they'd all been. There hadn't been much history in them, so to speak. Everyone had appeared to be a similar age in every photo; Eva was wearing the same tee-shirt in most of them (it was a Spiderman shirt); there weren't any of Lamar and his brother as boys, or of their parents, or of their graduation, or any of that kind of thing.

'Is that north?' Eva asked, pointing in the same direction I had.

I told her it was.

'And we can look there?'

'For what? The prison? I know exactly where it is.'

'No, not for the prison. For *the place*,' she said. 'You know.'

I did know, even if part of me wished I didn't. I told her we could look there if she really wanted to and she immediately started walking back down the hill, as though she was planning on going there right away. I was going to tell her what I'd thought about Lamar's pictures but it didn't look like she was interested in Lamar or his pictures any more.

There was a small creek trickling through the valley and Eva stopped by its banks and sat down on a boulder, un-shaded by the blackened branches of a grove of pines. On the other side of the creek a pink-red bed of fireweed was smouldering up the slopes of the opposite hill.

'You can sit here,' she said. 'There's plenty of boulder for the two of us.'

As we sat there we became aware of a twangy, crunchy noise coming from above us. It sounded like someone chewing peanut brittle and playing a Jew's harp at the same time. Once you'd become aware of it you couldn't block it out. On and on it went, the rhythm repetitive, relentless.

'What's that?' Eva asked.

'They're pine bugs.'

'I don't see them.'

'You can't, they're inside the trees.'

'What are they doing in there?'

'They're eating them.'

'Jesus! Even the wood isn't safe around here!' Eva said, looking down at all the bug bites on her arms and legs. There were a lot of them.

Across the creek we could see what I thought at first were other insects flitting amongst the fireweed blossoms.

'Whoopedy-fucking-doo-da, *another* kind of bug!' Eva said. 'What do those ones eat? Flowers? Small children?'

I tried to work out what bug they might be before I gradually realised they weren't bugs at all. They were small birds. They were hummingbirds.

'They're hummingbirds,' I said excitedly. There were so many. I'd never seen so many. Even from a distance they were beautiful; darting and hovering over the flowers, flitting in and out of sight as though the world were one huge magician's hat. I thought Eva would be as pleased as I was. It was a wonderful thing to see.

One, two, three ... I tried to count them but there were too many to count. Beyond the monotonous crunching of the pine bugs the air seemed to hold what I couldn't quite hear: the delicate zip and thrum of their wings.

'You can almost hear them,' I said, turning to Eva. But she wasn't there.

Up ahead I could see the ash-smudged white of her dress disappearing through the burn.

The Pukak

'What can you see down there?'

'Mostly weeds,' I said. 'And some shiners and other minnows. And some bugs … and there was a pike here earlier too. But mostly weeds,' I said, rambling. I was embarrassed about not knowing the proper names for anything, as I assumed she did. I was sitting on the shore of Wannigan Bay.

'Do you mind if I join you for a bit?'

'Sure,' I said.

Judith sat beside me and nestled herself down into the sand a few inches.

'Do you like fishing?' she asked. My fishing rod was lying a few feet away on the sand.

'I do. But I like just looking too.'

And then we both stared into the water.

'It's beautiful down there,' she said after a while.

At first I'd thought her sitting beside me would be an interruption, but it wasn't. Beneath the surface of the water everything stayed as it had been before. With her big white arms and blonde ponytail she looked as clean and clear as the winter she studied. Up close she smelt like a new bar of soap.

'I'm sorry about your husband,' I said.

'That's sweet of you. But really, there's nothing to be sorry about.'

I felt so calm and comfortable I couldn't shut myself up.

'Why are you getting divorced?'

'Oh, there're lots of reasons.'

'Like what?'

Judith looked up from the water and smiled at me, as if she was about to gently change the subject, and then she shrugged and looked back down.

'You know, I think he hated me sometimes.'

'Why?'

'I think a lot of the time he wanted me to be something else.'

'What did he want you to be?'

'About a foot shorter, for a start,' she said and began to laugh.

For a while then we said nothing. We just looked at the water.

'If I look down there for long enough it's like being somewhere else,' I said.

'I know exactly what you mean.'

'Is it the same with the thing you study? The beneath-the-snow thing?'

'The pukak. Yes, I guess it is a bit like that. Except of course I can't look at it so easily.'

'If you could, what would it look like?'

'Oh, there'd be columns of ice and snow and openings and tunnels. If you were small enough to get down there I imagine it'd be a bit like travelling through a frosty subway system. Not that you'd be able to see much, not with our eyes. In the day you'd hardly be aware of the sun at all, only a kind of soft, bluish glow.'

'And what lives down there?'

'It's really an incredibly rich and varied habitat...' she began, and then pulled herself up with a half smile. 'Mostly shrews and voles,' she continued. 'Plus the odd weasel or two. But mostly shrews and voles.'

As she was speaking some chippings began falling down the bank from the tracks. It was my father. He was skidding and stumbling his way towards us. I couldn't have been more surprised if I'd found a sasquatch there. He never came out this way. My mother had often taken me to Wannigan Bay when I was a child and I think – in some vague way – he still considered it our private place.

'Please, don't let me interrupt,' he said. 'I just came to check up on Zack.'

My father had never once checked up on me while I was pike fishing.

'Shrews and voles, you were saying.'

I knew then he'd been up by the tracks for a while. How long he'd been there for I didn't know, but we still had to have the same conversation all over again so he could pretend he'd not overheard the first one.

After about ten minutes it was me who felt like they were overhearing a conversation. My father and Judith were sitting on either side of me, talking about the difference between above and below the snow.

'The scale is entirely different down there,' Judith said. 'A shrew is a major predator. A fallen tree can be the limit of the world.'

'And I never even knew it existed,' my father said, shaking his head.

I noticed Judith had stopped trying to inch herself down into the sand and my father no longer looked like he was trying to swat a horsefly in front of his nose.

I hadn't said a word for a long time. Every few minutes I tried edging my way over towards my fishing rod.

'Oh, don't go,' they both kept saying whenever I did.

My father and Judith were talking about something called the

93

Heimal threshold, and I was beginning to think I might end up sitting between them on the sand forever, when my father's face went through several different alterations at once. His brows knitted together. His skin turned a kind of grey-white. Involuntarily, his front teeth slipped over his bottom lip and bit down on it.

Behind Judith's shoulder a figure had emerged on the tracks, where they curved around the far shore of the bay. For most of the curve they were hidden behind a line of trees but in two places they hugged the shore so closely they were visible. The first of these was quite a distance away but was still close enough for you to clearly make out the figure as a person. You could also see they had long red hair.

By the time they'd reached the second place, a hundred yards or so closer to us, you could also make out they were wearing a purple dress. It fluttered this way and that as its wearer walked in tightrope fashion along one of the tracks. My father hadn't spoken the whole while. He was staring intently at the figure, his mouth half open, almost as if he'd had a small stroke.

'Is there something wrong, Mr Taylor?' Judith asked.

'My apologies,' he spluttered abruptly. 'I'd better be getting home.'

'Oh,' said Judith.

But by then he was already clambering back up the bank.

Judith and I watched him lurch hurriedly alongside the tracks towards the cabin, each stride falling awkwardly in the gaps between the sleepers. Then we turned back to watch the figure approaching from the other direction.

'Do you know who that is?' she asked.

'That's Eva Spiller,' I said.

She was wearing a red wig. I'd not really noticed before but I did now: it was exactly the same colour as my mother's hair.

That night, before I went to sleep, I snuck out of my room to look at my father's notebook. I flicked through its pages until my flashlight illuminated the latest entry. It was from Samuel Hearne's account of his attempt to find the Coppermine River. He was discussing the effects of starvation.

'Besides, for want of action, the stomach so far loses its digestive powers, that after long fasting it resumes its office with pain and reluctance. During this journey I have too frequently experienced the dreadful effects of this calamity, and more than once been reduced to so low a state by hunger and fatigue, that when Providence threw anything in my way, my stomach has scarcely been able to retain more than two or three ounces, without producing the most oppressive pain.'

Three Day Blow

The next day was the last day of school but my father didn't
drop me off to catch the bus. He didn't say anything; when
we came to the end of the logging road he just carried on
driving. A few miles down the highway we passed Freddie
waiting at the end of his track. He looked up hopefully for a
moment as we approached, but then looked right back down
at his feet when he realised we weren't the bus, and Eva
wasn't with us (she'd only gone the once). In the rear-view
mirror I watched him disappear in a cloud of dust.

For two days there'd been no cloud in the sky and a hot,
dry wind had been blowing in from the west, from the
prairies. My mother had called these three-day blows, and
that name, together with the exotic origins and special scent
of the wind – a mixture of pine pitch and parched grass and
the smoke of unseen forest fires – had given it an almost
mythical quality to my younger mind, like the reign of
dragons, or their lairs, or their breath. She'd said the blow was
the weather's mind at work, deciding what it would be, and
that until it did it could be anything. As a child I'd often
imagined that if I walked far enough along the railway tracks
into this wind, towards the west, I'd end up in another
country, in some place I'd not even known existed. I was
about ten before I realised it'd probably end up being
Winnipeg.

Outside the truck window a chirruping din filled the air. In
the beaver ponds and road-side puddles the frogs were

getting noisy and restless. There was a panicky note in their voices. The three-day blow was dropping the water levels. So much around here depended on the transformations of water – freeze, thaw, flood, evaporation. They were better guides to the year than the names of seasons.

And then the voices suddenly vanished. All the other sounds did too. Without warning, my father had turned down the old track towards the swamp house. I felt like the frogs; as though the medium of my world was changing, was dropping perilously backwards and downwards. My voice would have been as panicky as theirs if I'd said anything, but I couldn't. My father remained as silent as me.

The track was in no shape at all. It was barely a track any more. We crashed through some saplings until we came to a blown-down poplar and had to stop the truck and walk. A few used shotgun cartridges were strewn on the deeply rutted gravel, left there by grouse hunters, and in some inexplicable gesture of housekeeping I tidied them away into my pocket. My father didn't notice them. They weren't the sort of thing he noticed.

The swamp, as far as I could tell, had moved at least fifteen feet closer to the house. My father had once planted a few lilacs out in front, around the area where the deck would have been, had it ever been completed. This, as it now turned out, had been his one successful piece of gardening; they'd grown thickly into bushes; the air was heavy with the scent of their blossoms. But the swamp had already begun to over-run the furthest out of these bushes. You could see their spindled tops reaching thinly out of the brown water.

As if to accommodate the expanding waters of the swamp, the house itself had shrunk. To an extent this must have just been the optical illusion or adjustment that attends all returns to childhood homes, but in this case there had also been an actual physical diminishment: a fallen poplar had flattened the small extension which had once housed my room. Elsewhere, the poplars and alders were already crowding around it, jostling it back into the bush.

I tried to think of significant dates, birthdays, anniversaries – reasons my father should choose this day to come back here as opposed to any other. But I couldn't think of any.

'Do you want to come in?' he asked. It was the first thing he'd said since we'd turned off the highway. He was stooping to look through the front doorway (the door itself had long since been wrenched off its hinges).

'I don't want to,' I said in a voice that sounded strange to me, that was somehow at once too small and too large for my mouth. I didn't want to go into the house. Like the alders and poplars, I wanted it to be ushered as quickly as possible back into the realms of a vegetable kingdom. I wished it only the swiftest of ruins. And in some ways I'm sure that wish has come true. There is a good chance not a single part of it remains these days, or at least no visible one.

What does remain is the image of my father stooping awkwardly through its absurdly small-looking door. I can't remember a time when he fitted easily into anywhere. He was constantly bumping his head on ceilings and door jambs, or else stubbing his toes on chairs and tables that seemed, miraculously, to have altered their positions and jumped in front of him. Our cupboards took a fearful beating from stray elbows. When he walked into a classroom the pupils at the front would surreptitiously move their desks a few inches backwards.

I sometimes imagined a time, before we moved up here, when my father had glided effortlessly through a world that was perfectly in proportion to him – or at least that he was perfectly in proportion to. I had few memories of our life before we'd moved, and no clear ones, and so the basis for this thought must have been a photograph that once sat on a dresser in the swamp house (whether it was still in there that day I have no idea). In this photograph he was standing outside Hart House in Toronto, dressed in something tidily creased and tweedy. My mother wasn't in the picture; it was her that had taken it, and perhaps this explained his pleased, rather goofy, smile. In most ways he looked exactly the same as I remember him, with his thick round glasses and high forehead and wispy brown hair, but he also – in a way it has taken me many years to put my finger on – looked entirely different. He looked, and I can think of no better or more exact way to put this, in place.

Of course, in one sense he was. He'd been born and bred in Toronto, the only son of a once well-to-do merchant family whose fortunes had steadily deteriorated as he'd grown up. There'd been enough left to put him through college, and then to start work on a post-graduate degree in history. I often imagine him tucked away in the carrel of the library, sifting through the records of trade exports and tariffs like some dusty, ink-fingered chronicler of an ebbing empire, pondering the roots of his family's decline. It was during this period that his parents died – in a yachting accident of all things – the one last hazard of their disappearing wealth and gentility. It was also when he'd met my mother, who was working as a trainee in the college library.

But it was more than just him being on familiar ground. In that photograph there was something comfortable, confident, even slyly jaunty, about him – in the way he stood, how his arms were folded, the angle of his chin. And yet whenever I picture him in the swamp house or the cabin at Sitting Down Lake it's as though he's been stuffed into a frame that doesn't quite fit. He's forever trying, and mostly failing, to find some quiet, uncluttered corner to accommodate his long, gangly self. He looks like a shy and gentle spider, suddenly exposed, trying to scuttle into some new place of safety.

While he was inside I closed my eyes and let the wind blow on my face. I tried to picture all the places I'd go to if I could. I pictured corral islands and mountain ranges, jungles and deserts, I even tried to imagine looking out from the lighthouse in Lamar's photo at the slate-blue and endless ocean, but try as I might the swamp kept creeping up to the edge of whatever landscape I conjured. And when I opened my eyes, there it was. The three-day blow hadn't evaporated a molecule of it.

My room, crushed beneath the poplar, wasn't the only one that had disappeared. There was another missing, although that had been missing for many years. After my mother died my father had dismantled the bathroom, taking down each panel of the insulation siding before removing it plank by plank, tile by tile, board by board. It wasn't such a huge alteration. The room itself had only been added – as had my bedroom – as a kind of annex to the original building (there was already a small shower and toilet off the kitchen). Unlike the sculptures, he hadn't thrown these boards and planks into the swamp and their remains lay over to the left of the lilac bushes. They were still visible there, although so heaped now with shed needles and leaves and dead branches they seemed to bulge above the earth like some ancient and mysterious mound or dolmen.

The interior of this bathroom has long since become obscure to me; it is murky and flecked in my memory, as though it was a berth in a shipwreck being entered by a diver. As for the door into it, well that is another matter. After my father had dismantled the room the door remained. It was almost directly opposite the front entrance and was one of the first things you saw when you came in. To this day, I don't know if he ever sealed or nailed it shut. I never tried the handle to check. But I sometimes imagined the surprise of some visitor, opening it and finding themselves staring directly out at the woods and the swamp. Perhaps it was a good thing we didn't have any visitors.

I remember the last time I saw it when it still led into a room. It would have been late in the winter, towards the middle of March, a month or so before ice-out. It was a school day. That morning our class had been taken down to the river where Mr Strum, under his occasional guise of outdoor safety instructor (otherwise we knew him best as the owner of the town's gas station) spent at least half an hour walking up and down the bank, shoving his leg through the needling ice for our edification.

'You see,' he kept saying.

We all saw. And to make things even clearer he then launched into his extensive, and well-aired, repertoire of drowned children stories. It often seemed a wonder to us after these lessons that any children from Crooked River had ever managed to grow up.

We'd reached the bridge near the town museum when someone let out a cry and began pointing across to the far bank. Mr Strum took his leg out of the river and looked over. We all did.

There it was, just to the edge of some frost-bent reeds: a duck. This duck had been frozen into the ice. The snow must have melted enough that week to reveal it. While its head, thankfully, was bent downwards and embedded out of sight below the surface of the ice, its tail feathers were sticking up above it, as though the freeze had caught it unawares as it surveyed the river's bed. It must have been there since

December. There was no telling whether it had been injured and unable to fly or if the ice – which had come suddenly that year – had indeed trapped it. We broke out into the usual children's chorus; a mixture of giggles, sighs of muted sympathy, exclamations of curiosity, questions. Seeing no way to incorporate it into his lesson – which after all was about the ice's treacherous fragility – Mr Strum simply observed 'That's one unlucky duck' and ushered us quickly past it and further along the river bank.

Or most of us, at least. I lingered there for a good while longer, staring at the duck, long enough for Mr Strum to have to return and lead me back to join the rest of the class. I saw it then, as I have seen it since, as an ill and unfortunate omen.

By some twist of irony or cruelty or chance, we actually spent that afternoon in the library. We'd been meant to have some after-school reading event or other but the person meant to lead it never showed up and so we'd ended up just milling about the place. Mr McKinnon, my mother's boss (it wasn't one of the days she worked), had taken great pains to acknowledge our connection by taking me aside and pointing out various shelves of natural history books. He must have assumed I shared my mother's interests.

There was one in particular that caught my attention, called 'Creatures of Fancy' or some such thing. It was about legendary animals and the real ones that had possibly inspired them. It worked mainly, as far as I can recall, by juxtaposition. So, for example, on one page it had a slightly comical illustration of sailors spying on mermaids and a man in a medieval smock selling a unicorn's horn, while on the page opposite there were photographs of a manatee and a narwhal. I was still looking through this book when, eventually, my father arrived. He'd arranged to pick me up on his way back from the school.

There would, I suppose, have been an hour or so of daylight left, although the cloud had got progressively thicker during the day and it was already quite gloomy. We drove down the street flanked by mounds of snow that had, by this time of the year, grown into almost unfeasibly huge piles, as though the whole visible town had been dug out of it, like an ancient city excavated out of mud. This snow was depressingly pocked and dirty; a chimney-sweep's face sort of snow – coated with salt and oil and exhaust smoke.

When we got back to the swamp house I went immediately to check on the two bird feeders my mother had set up near the edge of the swamp that winter. As the birds had slowly started to return she'd begun giving me a nickel for each new kind I spotted. I didn't see any that day. I looked for about fifteen or so minutes before giving up and heading back to the house.

I was surprised to find my father sitting out on the boards of our unfinished deck. He gestured for me to join him and so I did. I must have asked him something but he didn't reply. How long we sat there for I'm not sure. He kept staring at the deck.

'I never finished it,' he said eventually, running his hand along the boards.

That was the only thing I remember him saying before the ambulance and police car arrived minutes later.

As one of the officers led me away to his car (my father was waiting by the ambulance) I broke away from him and ran towards our front door. I must have reached it because I remember prising it open before he managed to grab hold of me. For a few seconds I stood on the threshold. The living room was as it always was: the table in the centre, the orangey brown Chesterfield beneath the window, the giant moose rack on the wall with its tines tapering away into strange creatures. On the far side of it the bathroom door was closed.

103

And that is all. It was no more than a few seconds before I was led away. And yet – and I don't know if I felt it then, or if it was something I began to feel afterwards – as I stood there looking in I was sure that if it had been one second more I would have begun to feel ice beginning to form and harden around my neck.

My father couldn't have been inside the house for more than about half an hour but it felt much longer. It was as if I'd been transported back to those long sad days I'd once felt I might never get out of. When eventually he did come out he was carrying a cribbage board, a rusty pancake griddle, and a musty old blanket with a picture of a sunrise woven into it, which was now so grimy with black mould spores it looked like after sunset. He placed these reverently on the ground beside the lilac bushes and sat down beside them.

'Do you remember this?' he asked, picking up the cribbage board. 'Fifteen two and that'll do. Fifteen four and then no more. Fifteen six and that's a fix.' I could feel the alarm beginning to rise up through my stomach and press queasily against my sternum. Of course I remembered the board. Of course I remembered the words. They were the rhymes my parents had used when they'd played. I didn't say anything.

He was smiling in a crooked, slightly wide-eyed way, the way people do when they're trying to assure you everything's normal when it isn't. And this wasn't. My father and I didn't talk about things like this. My mother had taken nostalgia away with her. She'd made it dangerous. It wasn't something we allowed ourselves.

He patted the ground beside him and I sat uncomfortably down. 'I don't know if they even make these blankets anymore,' he said, fingering the mouldy wool of the sunrise. He kept running his other hand through his thin hair. Strands of it were sticking up, as though alarmed by the sudden attention.

It was as if he was trying to pretend we'd discovered an old trunk in our family attic and were sorting fondly through its contents. Ah, look at this sweater. Do you remember wearing it? A wooden tennis racquet, a gramophone. Can you believe we used to use this stuff? I tried my best to play along. But just as my attempts to conjure deserts and jungles had failed earlier, so now did my ability to see what was in front of me any other way. It was what it was. We were sitting in front of a rusty pancake griddle and some old blanket and a board with one hundred and twenty holes in it.

What it was my father was seeing I have no idea. After about twenty minutes he jumped abruptly up and began throwing them into the swamp.

'Fuck,' he shouted, hurling in the cribbage board. 'Fuck, fuck, fuck,' he shouted and the blanket and pancake griddle were gone. 'Fuck, fuck, fuck,' he shouted and started pulling up the lilac bushes and throwing them. 'Why did you bring me here? Where the fuck did you go?' I'd never heard him swear before. I never would again.

Afterwards he knelt at the edge of the swamp.

'I'm sorry,' he said.

I couldn't tell whether he was speaking to me or to the things he'd thrown or to my mother or to the water itself.

North by North-West

'What do you think?' Eva asked.

'Where'd you get that?'

'My uncle's got loads of weird shit lying around.'

'The bugs will eat you alive.'

'Oh, Zachary Taylor,' she said, putting on a southern accent and glancing big-eyed at me over her shoulder, 'isn't that just what a lady likes to hear.'

She was wearing a pith helmet and a pair of baggy beige shorts.

'We better get going.'

'Yes, sir!' she said, saluting. 'Time and leeches wait for no man, sir!'

I was beginning to wonder if it was such a good idea taking her.

On the way out we passed Lamar, who was by the banks of the creek hammering away at a wooden frame made with two-by-fours. The sun hadn't even touched the horizon yet.

'Another No Trespassing sign?' I asked.

'Don't ask,' Eva said.

The Oldsmobile was parked over by the far side of the cabin. I didn't ask about that either.

'It's like Avalon,' Eva said as we made our way along the shore.

I'd never imagined the lake that way but I could see how you could. The three-day blow had passed and it was as still and flat as I'd ever seen it. Out past our dock a solitary loon dipped smoothly below the surface and such was the silence and stillness I could hear the faint splash of its dive and see the ripples circling out into the bay. A mist hung over the water, snaking up in slow, hushed swirls and eddies. Eva was right. On a morning like this you could half believe in secret worlds and hidden borders, passages into other dimensions.

'That's the Toad,' I said as we passed the rock at the end of the point.

'Pleased to meet you, Mr Toad,' she said.

When we arrived, the mist was still hanging over the shaded ground beneath Oskar's place.

'What's with the tree house?'

'It's a Finnish thing,' I said.

'Holy shit, what's with that?' Eva said as we passed beneath the first bear skull.

'It's a Finnish thing.'

'Don't tell me,' she said as we came in sight of the second, 'it's a Finnish thing.'

Oskar wasn't up and I didn't knock. The day before he'd told me I could check the traps on my own. I hadn't mentioned anything about taking Eva.

It took me about twenty pulls to get the engine going and when it did its sickly mechanical splutter limped all the way across the lake and came back in wheezy echoes. Avalon was going to take a while to cross. Eva was sitting up in the bow seat, facing me. Once we got moving she took the pith helmet off. Her hair was black and straight and fell in short bangs across her forehead. The breeze from the boat flipped it up into little waves and curls.

'What direction are we headed in, skipper?'

'North by north-west, more or less,' I said.

'Like the film?'

'What film?'

Eva mouthed something at me but I couldn't hear what she was saying. At first I thought it was the noise of the engine drowning her out but then I realised she wasn't actually using her voice. She was miming.

'You know, *that* film,' she finally said.

I didn't know. We'd never had a television. Sometimes they played a film at the Native Friendship Centre in Crooked River. You could tell when there was one playing because there were cigarette breaks every half an hour and everyone would be out on the sidewalk smoking.

'I'm on the shark's side, one hundred per cent,' I'd heard someone say once.

'Oh yeah, that one,' I said. I didn't want Eva knowing how little I knew about those things.

'It's like opening letters,' Eva said.

'I guess it is,' I said, unfolding the aluminium trap and dropping the leeches into the tote.

'Can you imagine getting one? Oh, great, look what they've sent me – another batch of leeches!' Eva had been in high spirits the whole journey out. As we'd crossed the lake she'd leaned over the side of the boat and let her fingers slip along the surface of the water. They left the tiniest of wakes behind them.

Around the edges of the pond you could see the purple of irises. About a foot more of the beaver's lodge was visible. The old wood piled on top of it was as smooth and pale as bone. I remembered to reset the traps at different levels. When I'd finished we landed and I took Eva to see the prison.

'This is it?' she said.

'This is it,' I said.

'I don't know. I was expecting something, you know, more prison-y.'

I looked around. She was right. As ruins went, it wasn't very anything. 'This is probably where the prisoners slept,' I said, pointing to the mouldering logs. 'And this is probably where they cooked.'

I didn't understand myself. Last time I'd been here I hadn't wanted it to be a prison at all. Now I was trying to show how it had been.

'I'm sorry,' I said, for reasons that were beyond me.

'For what,' she said. She took her camera out and started taking pictures.

The two burrs on the birch tree bulged out at me like eyeballs.

By the time Eva found the old wood stove any hint of disappointment had disappeared. She knelt down to photograph the inside of it.

'Do you think this ash is from back then? It could be historical ash.'

'I don't know.'

'Do you think any of them escaped?'

'I don't know. I guess they could have. There weren't many guards.'

'I bet at least one of them did.'

After taking pictures of the rusty kettle Eva announced that she'd found a key.

'See,' she said. 'To open their handcuffs with or something. Or the door.'

It looked an awful lot like a fork to me. 'I don't think they were locked in,' I said. Eva didn't take any notice.

'I knew it. What do you think his name was? Gunther. Yes,

I think that was his name. Ver is Gunther? Gunther ist eskapen.

'You don't speak German, do you?'

Eva started marching between the trees. 'Mein Gott! Herr Gunther ist goner.'

Beyond the site of the prison was a narrow ridge of naked bedrock. My father had made me some baloney sandwiches for lunch and, before heading back, we clambered up to the top of it to eat them. On one side you could see the beaver pond, on the other a creek snaked its way through the bush, flanked by the lighter, swampy green of reeds and bulrushes.

'He must have gone that way,' Eva said after we'd finished eating.

'Who?'

'Poor Gunther,' she said, sounding genuinely stricken over the plight of her imaginary soldier. 'It was tough going but I'm sure he made it in the end.' She lit a green death and blew the smoke up towards the sky. Then she turned to face me and asked: 'And which way will we go next time?'

To reach where, I was about to ask. For most of the trip I'd tried to forget the main reason she'd come with me. Part of me hoped she'd lost interest in the whole idea.

'You mean to reach the Un-named Water Body?' I said.

She nodded her head.

'We'll probably go up that way too,' I said, allowing Gunther an existence despite myself.

Eva fixed her eyes intently on the creek, as though she could navigate it by looking alone and had already travelled far beyond the portion of it which was visible to us. And even though the morning's mist had long evaporated you could almost believe it could lead to any place you wanted – to

Gunther's home, to the source of the three-day blow, to anywhere at all. Or at least you could for a second or two.

'When?'

Not for a long time, I hoped.

Trains

Later that day Oskar and I walked down the tracks past Wannigan Bay to the Switch Ponds to set some minnow traps. They were called the Switch Ponds because of the rail switch beside the culvert that separated them. On our way there I'd made sure to give this switch a wide berth, worried it might clamp shut on my foot and trap me on the tracks like one of those women in black and white films.

On the way back we talked about leeches. I was asking Oskar where they went in the winter. I wanted to know if, beneath the ice, the lake became a kind of water pukak; if – beyond our sight – the summer version of it was dismantled like scenery behind a curtain and a winter version erected its place.

Oskar said he wasn't sure what the leeches did in the winter. He said with no fresh blood on offer they probably just curled up somewhere and went to sleep like bears. But he didn't know for certain. Sometimes the leeches were a mystery to him. In fact, they were often a mystery to him.

How different was it for the rest of the lake under the ice, I asked? He said I should have a good enough idea of that from ice fishing: that in the shallower parts it was colder and darker and most of the warmer water fish were sluggish and not doing much of anything. As for the trout, and the other fish that liked the cold and the deep, they just carried on as usual. At a certain depth the lake probably didn't change much at all, whatever season it was.

We'd made it past the wannigans and were close to the culvert at Butterfly Creek. Out on his lawn, Lamar was hammering boards onto a frame. It wasn't quite square or round, more a kind of hexagon.

'What do you think he's building?' I asked.

'Lamar is Lamar,' Oskar said, which is what he usually said when I asked him something about Lamar.

'Was he different before?'

Oskar crushed a horsefly on his neck.

'Before what?'

'Before the accident,' I said.

'He is what he is now,' he said, stopping and crouching down on his haunches. He felt the track with his hand. 'There's a train coming,' he said. And without another word we both moved off to the edge of the chippings and continued on our way.

We'd made it past the Burn before we heard its whistle. We were almost at the path leading down to my cabin when the engine shrieked and shuddered its way around the bend. Moving off a few feet towards an outcrop of granite, as though subconsciously seeking the safer ground, we stopped to watch it pass.

It's as if the approaching commotion of that train, the screech of its brakes and the blare of its whistle (so soulful and melancholy from afar, so shocking and loud up close), have shaken loose my memories of the next few minutes; they judder by in stops and starts, in jumps and tremors. It was a long train, and these longer trains had to slow right down as they hugged the bends and curves of the lake's shore. The trucks went by, one by one by one in what felt like endless succession, marked with ears of wheat, painted yellow and a baked, dusty red, the colour of plains and savannahs, and here and there decorated in sprays of bright graffiti that seemed, out here, to have been formed out of an entirely different alphabet – an outlandish and colourful hieroglyphics. It stretched further and further around the lake's shore until it was like some huge python encircling it. By this time it'd slowed to almost a walking pace.

Eva was about two hundred yards in front of us when I first spotted her, standing near the edge of the Burn. She was wearing some kind of ancient poncho and looked raggedly triangular, like the top of a spruce tree. She nodded as each truck rumbled past, as if she was counting them. I called out to her but my voice was swallowed up by the train.

'That's Lamar's niece,' I shouted to Oskar, which seemed immediately rather pointless – it couldn't really be anybody else. He didn't reply and turning to face him I found he was staring at Eva. His skin had become terribly pale, intensifying the blackness of his eyes and making it appear as though they were reflecting the charred surface of the Burn. I looked back at Eva. She was still nodding her head. She was at least three or four steps closer to the train, close enough for the agitated air to lift up her brown curls and blow them across her face.

Oskar was standing beside me and then he was running towards her. He was silent and then his mouth was open and moving, although the sounds and words it made are lost. And then I was running too. I caught up to him and grabbed hold of his sleeve. I had no idea why I was doing this – I had no idea what he was intending to do; it was as though I was impelled by some kind of skittery, panicked unease or instinct, the type that makes animals bolt through gates and jump fences. By the time I'd caught up to him, Oskar's baseball cap had flown off, leaving his hair sticking up in strands here and there as if the air had become electrified. He shook me off in one movement – with a physical strength I'd

114

never suspected and which made him appear suddenly bigger – and began to run again. At that moment Eva turned, looked at us, smiled, and then, in two athletic bounds, stepped between two of the passing trucks and vanished.

It was a long wait. The thumping, rhythmic progress of the trucks seemed to count it out like some giant and deafening metronome. I remember watching the painted ears of wheat whooshing by, and Oskar standing a few yards in front of me where he'd come to a stop, looking as small as a child now, trembling, his pale face and black eyes pointed anxiously down towards the cinders. The trucks passed by, the other side of the tracks briefly visible in the gaps between them; the lake was there and then it wasn't; one outcome was possible and then another – a double-sided card flipped back and forth. And then, just when it seemed there would be no end to it, the red of the caboose flashed by. I could hear crickets again. Eva was standing on the other side of the tracks calmly smoking a green death. As we stared at her, she stubbed it out and started heading back in the direction of Butterfly Creek. And in the slow diminuendo, as the rumble of the train ebbed away into the humming of the tracks, and the screeching of its brakes became distant groans, Oskar turned back towards me, picked up his hat and, without a word, walked away into the Burn.

North by North-West II

He wasn't in his cabin the next morning and his boat was still tied to the dock. I looked out back around the wood pile; I checked behind the Toad. Then I walked the tracks all the way out to the Switch Ponds, searching the verges, stopping to look in the wannigans. I even forced myself to glance over the Burn. Usually, Oskar's nature sleeps didn't worry me (he'd been having them a long time before I was around) but this time felt different. I could picture how pale his face had been the day before; the ruddy darkness of his skin as horribly blanched as his bears' skulls. He must have seen her in Eva.

When I returned to his cabin he still wasn't there. I left a note on his door saying I'd check the leeches. Then, halfway along the trail to my cabin I turned around, went back, and left another note saying I'd check the minnow traps too. Then I stomped my way over to Butterfly Creek.

Outside on the lawn, Lamar was still hammering away at his timber frame. It looked like some kind of tower now. He nodded as I walked past but didn't stop hammering. I might have asked him what it was but I guess we'd already reached the high water mark in our conversation.

Eva opened the front door, wearing the same pith helmet and beige shorts as she had the previous morning.

'Why did you do that?' I demanded.

'Why did I do what?' she said with an infuriatingly straight face.

116

'You know.'

'Oh, you mean my little trick with the train,' she said, and smiled.

Behind her I could see two moose peering at me from the wall of dead animals. I had a sudden urge to rush in and punch one of them on the nose. Moose, I thought, had very punch-able noses.

'It wasn't a trick. It was dangerous. It was stupid.'

I had a lot more to say but it felt as though my tongue had swollen up and was too big for my mouth. It was what often happened in my dreams, even the ones that weren't nightmares.

'Why'd your leech buddy freak out?'

'His name's Oskar.'

'Was it a Finnish thing?'

It was hopeless me trying to explain. Everything I wanted to say was clogged up in my head like a sinus infection. There was a painful pressure in my forehead.

'It was dangerous. It was…'

'Look, okay. No need to go on about it. I was lucky. What can I say, I'm lucky.'

'You weren't lucky. It was dangerous. It was stupid.'

'Why are you crying, Zachary?'

'I'm not crying.'

'It sure looks like it.'

'I'm not,' I sniffled. I felt like throwing her in the lake.

'When can we go to the un-named water body?' she asked suddenly.

'We could go today,' I said huffily, glad the subject had changed. 'We could go right now.'

The next thing I knew we were out on the water, headed north by north-west. It wasn't what I'd planned that morning. It didn't once occur to me that Eva hadn't even needed to get changed.

117

The creek we'd looked at the day before petered out after about two or three kilometres, falling first into a rocky shallows and then into a weedy marsh.

'What do we do now?' Eva asked after we'd pulled the boat up.

'We'll bushwhack it,' I said, looking at her map with its red dots and holes and trying to sound authoritative. I didn't feel that way. I knew it was difficult to move that far through the bush without a trail or a river to follow; more difficult still to find something in it. A map will only give you so much when you're standing in a forest: a direction – maybe; a destination – a considerably bigger maybe. If I'd learnt anything from my father's notebooks and the walls of our school it was that now was a good time to pack up and head home. I imagined us starving or freezing or being eaten by bears, or else wandering forever in gloomy green circles like unhappy wood spirits. And yet I still walked right on into it, and the queasy feeling in my stomach wasn't all dread.

In looking at illustrations of other forests – in books and magazines – I'd often been struck by how enviably open and accessible they appeared. The trees would be generously spaced, the ground beneath them pleasantly shaded and clear; somewhere you might stroll leisurely on a carpet of grass, stopping to smell a flower or two, a deer ambling easily past. (Of course at night, or when the story had taken a more twilit turn, it was different.) But the forest I knew, or knew a little of at least, had never been like this. When you entered it, you weren't walking along *in* a forest, you were clambering and pushing and crawling and stumbling through and over and around and under it. It was a place of obstacles, of hydra-headed opposition. Past one there was always another: the blow-down, the deadfall, the alder and balsam saplings, the thickly bunched young pines, the

118

skinny, witch-fingered spruce boughs, the sphagnum-covered bogs, the swamps, the granite boulders and slabs. In there you could barely think beyond the next footstep you had to make, the next encounter. And all the time, beyond it, there it was, that feeling – jagged and darkly glittering like shattered obsidian: the fear of being lost; the strange, sharp, unexpected joy of being in a place where being truly lost was possible.

For half an hour, then an hour, Eva and I crashed and blundered our way north. Sometimes a space would appear to open out beyond the trees in front of us.

'Do you see it? Is that it?'

'I don't know.'

'How far did it look on the map?'

'Further.'

'Fuck, how far is this?'

'This isn't far at all.'

'How did Gunther find his way through this shit?'

I snapped branches as we went, pushed over saplings. Hansel and Gretel had it almost right: make trails; the signs of where you've been may help you get back there. Behind me Eva moved recklessly forward, marking nothing.

And then, quite suddenly, without me even knowing we were close, we were there. I remember looking up and discovering there weren't any branches poking into my eyes. Two wood ducks were winging their way over me and beneath them the light was sparkling on water. A beaver turned and slapped his tail in admonition, the mosquitoes hummed and whined, and below the low twanging of a green frog was the sound of our hushed footsteps, approaching slowly and tentatively now, as if it were the first day of the creation.

'Jesus,' Eva exclaimed in disappointment. 'Is this it?'

'I think it is. I'm pretty sure it is.'

She brushed some twigs out of her hair and took a long hard look at it.

'It looks exactly the same as the last two beaver ponds we passed,' she said.

'What were you expecting,' I said.

'I don't know. The name hardly gives much away!'

She was right. It wasn't much to look at. It was barely bigger than a pond and had a single, stony island in its centre, and growing in the centre of this a single tree; a stunted, ragged-looking birch, hardly more than a shrub, that'd probably taken a thousand years to grow that big out of the three grains of dirt it had for its roots.

That was the last thing Eva said for a while. We searched the shoreline for about two hours and found nothing. I wasn't even sure what exactly it was we were meant to be looking for. Old wreckage, luggage? Bones? I didn't want to ask. We carried on this macabre beach-combing in silence.

Once we'd been around the entire shoreline Eva stopped and took off her pith helmet. She looked up at the sky and then around at the spindly spruces growing nearest us.

'This is useless,' she said.

I didn't say anything.

'Fucking useless,' she said and then started wading into the lake. She'd got in up to her thighs, and the water had soaked her beige shorts, when she leaned over, reached down into the water with her arms, and began parting the lily-pads and their stems as if they were curtains. Her black bangs were wet. Her nose was almost touching the surface. I didn't know what it was she wanted to see down there. I didn't follow her. The water was murky and tea-bag dark, like it was beneath the drop-off.

120

And then she started diving. She dove and dove until I could see she was running out of strength and breath. Her wig had come off. It was floating amongst the lily pads like a dead animal. Her real hair was cropped so short you could see the pale, exposed skin of her scalp.

'Hey,' I shouted. 'Why don't you rest for a bit?'

She didn't take any notice. Her head disappeared, resurfaced and then disappeared again.

'Hey,' I shouted, rolling up my pants and wading in up to my knees. The dark water sucked at the hairs on my shins. This time she resurfaced only a few feet away from me. She was breathing hard and her skin was a pale, sickly blue.

'Why don't you give it a break?'

'Why don't you fuck off,' she spluttered.

The next time she resurfaced there was water trickling out of the corner of her mouth. The water was up to her waist and her shorts and shirt were clinging heavily to her body. She could barely keep standing.

'Look,' I said, 'we can try again another…'

And then I stopped.

Whatever it was Eva was seeing and hearing in that moment it wasn't me – or not exactly me. She was staring blurrily ahead and, seemingly, straight through me. Her head had begun to sway and tilt and her gaze was oddly quizzical and dilatory, like a bird in slow motion eyeing some distant trinket or bauble. For a few seconds her lips appeared poised on the precarious edge of speaking, like somebody who was very drunk trying to say something without slurring; as if the words were obstacles and her breath an intricate and half-forgotten path around them.

'We can try…' I began again.

She looked directly at me and then to my right and then up

into the sky, as though she was trying to figure out where this voice was coming from, as though it was emanating weakly from another dimension – the whisper of a ghost; the mysterious knocking of a poltergeist. I was the shadow of a shadow. I was invisible. I wasn't even there.

I remembered then where I had seen this expression before. And for a second it was as if the sun had dropped out of the sky and the clammy green light that once fell through the windows of the swamp house was now falling here too. Why didn't she see me? Why didn't she hear me?

'Eva,' I shouted with as much breath as I could fit in my lungs. 'Eva, please!'

She went to dive under again. She only just had the strength to break the surface. But she seemed to find some extra when I reached over and tried to grab hold of her arm.

'Eva,' I shouted again.

She ripped her arm out of my grasp and then swung around and pushed me over. For a moment I floundered, shocked, the water lapping my chin, and then I pushed myself forward and grabbed hold of her waist. And then we were rolling around and around in the water. I caught glimpses of sky and leaf-litter and lily stems. I could see the island close to us, and its single lonely tree. And then it was just the murky, tea-black dark. I could taste the earthy rot of vegetation. We stopped rolling when I began throwing up the water I'd swallowed. It was Eva who hauled me ashore.

We'd ended up on the island. After I'd got my breath back, we sat down together between two small boulders. I leant against the one nearest me; its smooth granite surface had been cracked and fissured by the slow expansions and contractions of ice, by the transformations of water. We sat in silence for a long time. The sun was getting gradually lower.

Eva had rubbed the side of her neck so much it was bleeding. Her cropped hair was matted with mud and pond weed.

'What'll we call it?' I suddenly asked.

'What are you talking about?' Eva said. Her voice was softer now. She could see me.

'We should give it a name.'

'What?'

'The lake.'

'Why?'

'I don't know. That's just what you do – like with new ships and stuff like that.'

Eva looked at the water for a few minutes.

'Let's call it Hummingbird Lake,' she said.

'Why that?' I asked, assuming she'd say because of the ones we'd seen in the Burn.

And then for the first time, and the last too, Eva told me the story of how she was orphaned.

She'd lived in Winnipeg back then, she told me, although she only vaguely remembered what it'd been like there. Her family's house was close to the river, which you could see from the bottom of their back yard. It had a long porch, hung here and there with blankets that her mother made, with landscapes knitted into them, mostly lakes at sunrise and sunset. She remembered a loon silhouetted against a perfectly round yellow sun. Her father worked as a printer for the newspaper and came home each day smelling of ink. His fingernails were always slightly black, however many times he washed them.

Her best friend was Alfred Christianson, a boy with one leg slightly shorter than the other. He had a shoe with a block of wood nailed onto the heel.

She knew her grandparents – who'd died before she was

123

born – had lived somewhere over to the east. She knew her uncle still lived there. But she didn't know the name of the place. She only really knew it as 'there' – from her father's repeated use of the phrase 'The best thing I ever did was get out of there.'

Every year they went on a holiday with Lamar, who by then had lots of money but no family of his own. He'd plan these holidays months and months in advance. He'd think about them all through the fall and winter. Her father would often get off the phone in November and say things like, 'Lamar says we should keep July free. And do we like lobster.' They went to the Rockies, they went to British Columbia. They went to Peggy's Cove in Nova Scotia.

The first time they went to Crooked River as a family it was to go on a special trip Lamar had arranged for them. It was supposed to be something to make 'there' okay to come back to. They'd driven for eight hours, watching the edge of the prairie become the shield. Eva had sat on the back seat and fallen asleep counting trees. If you stay awake you might see a moose, her mother told her. But it was a long time to keep looking, even for a moose.

The Hummingbird was a float plane. It was used to take fishermen and hunters up to outpost cabins on lakes that were too remote to get to any other way. The Spillers were booked in for a week at a place whose name Eva couldn't remember, only that the pilot, who had a bushy red moustache and a baseball hat that said 'Ducks Unlimited', had told her it was a lake with sandy beaches and trout the size of her father's leg. 'In fact,' he'd added with a wink, 'some of them are pretty much the same size as you.'

He was showing them the plane. 'The make's a Beaver,' he told them, 'so I sort of changed her name – you know, to something that actually flies.'

On the door there was a small sticker of a hummingbird. It looked more like an insect than a bird.

'If you say so,' Eva's father said.

They were due to leave the next morning, weather permitting.

That night Eva dreamt of a huge trout pulling her into the water. Under the surface there was a giant insect with a proboscis as long as a swordfish's bill.

'I've been waiting for you,' it told her.

'It's cold down here,' Eva replied.

'It's always cold down here,' it said.

When she couldn't get back to sleep and went to get a glass of milk the floorboards creaked and her mother's voice came sleepily from behind a closed door.

'Just count to a hundred and if it's light by then you can get up,' she said.

It was what she told her when she got up too early on Christmas morning. But that wasn't the same as this. She didn't want the morning to come at all. She didn't want to go on the plane. She didn't want to go on the trip. She wanted to go straight back to Winnipeg and play street hockey with Alfred (which she always won), or operation (which she didn't mind losing).

But the morning did come. And worse – it was a fine, still morning, with the sun as perfect and yellow as one of the ones on her mother's blankets.

'You better get your butt in gear,' her father said while Eva dawdled over a bowl of Cheerios. 'Those trout aren't going to catch themselves.' She tried dawdling some more, lifting her spoon listlessly to her mouth, letting its contents drip back into the bowl.

The pilot was already waiting for them by the dock when

they arrived. He was weighing some of their supplies before loading them onto the plane.

'Hop on,' he said smiling, pointing down at the scales. 'You must be an eighty pounder, at least.'

'I'm not a fish,' Eva replied moodily.

'Whoa there, partner. Never said you were.'

'I'm not a cowboy either.'

The pilot lifted his eyebrows and went back to weighing the supplies.

Lamar had arranged it so his brother and his family would go on first and have a few hours to settle themselves in before he joined them. He waited at one end of the dock while Eva and her parents waited at the other. Her mother had tied a blue ribbon in her hair, to stop it blowing into her face when they were flying.

'Honey, I'm pretty sure they close the windows when they're flying,' her father had said.

'No harm wearing it just in case,' she said. 'I don't want to miss out on the view.'

'Think how far you'll be able to see from up there,' Eva's father said to her, pointing up into the cruelly blue sky.

She was beginning to feel like she might puke.

'Ladies first,' said the pilot.

Eva wasn't sure what exactly happened next. Some things stood out clear enough – her father trying to lift her into the plane, her legs kicking out, her lungs with no breath in them, her mother saying, 'Don't worry honey, she can come later, with Lamar' – but the rest was just random detail: her father's hand on her upper arm, the ink-blackened cuticles of his fingers standing out against the whiteness of her skin; the blue ribbon tying back her mother's hair; the pilot's red

126

moustache; the print of the duck's head on his hat. And even these were all jumbled, forever shifting and re-settling in her memory like crystals in a kalaidoscope. So occasionally when she remembered it, it was the pilot's cuticles that had the ink on them and it was her father who had his hair tied back with the blue ribbon; or it was her father who was wearing the duck hat and the pilot was wearing the ribbon. Sometimes her mother had a red moustache.

Then it became a scene. Her watching from the dock; an undulating line of trees at the edge of the calm water; the plane's engine spluttering as it taxied along the lake; its engine warming slowly up, growing louder and steadier; the burst of sudden speed and noise; the final departing kiss of the floats on the still water. And then the Hummingbird was arcing around the far shore, circling back to tip a wing at her before receding beyond the line of trees, the wake from the take-off slapping against the tyres nailed to the side of the dock, the waves getting smaller, the sound getting fainter.

Then it was just waiting; watching the same horizon from the dock – for one hour, for two hours, for three. And on the fourth Lamar appearing beside her, his hands shaking, his eyes looking in disbelief at the same horizon, as though it were not meant to be there, and then leading her into a small office where moose heads peered down at her and huge trout and pike stared past her with glazed eyes, offering the faint but clear premonition that she'd been dragged abruptly out of one element and would have to learn quickly how to live in another one. And then Lamar banging his head on the wall until his forehead bled and a woman from the office leading her outside saying, 'Something bad has happened honey, something terrible has happened.'

Eva picked up a stone and flung it through the branches of the little birch into the lake.

'I should have been on it,' she said bitterly. 'I was a coward.'

'You were only a kid,' I said. 'You were lucky you weren't on it.'

'That's what everyone told me,' she said. 'And that's what everyone who knows about it still tells me – and if they don't say it then that's what they're thinking: she's the lucky one. But most of the time I don't feel lucky. And sometimes I do stuff, as a kind of test, to see if I am.'

She picked up another rock and threw it.

'Because sometimes I wish I had been on it, you know. Sometimes I have these thoughts and I can't bear it that I wasn't.'

I didn't know what to say. I looked at the circles expanding outwards from the spot where the rock had landed, moving slowly towards the lonely shore. There was no way of knowing if this was the place or not, no way at all. But for the first time I think I started to understand why she wanted it to be. And I began to wish then that she could have found something, anything at all.

On the way back we hardly spoke. The light was failing and around us in the bush were those sounds of twigs snapping that move your heart and feet a bit faster. This time Eva was more careful. I saw her break some branches and stop now and again to look around.

When we got back she climbed up onto the ridge overlooking the prison site and the creek. In the failing light you could barely make out the remains of the wall or the stove or anything else. The creek no longer appeared as if it could lead anywhere.

'At least Gunther made it,' she said.

She sounded glad, as glad as if he'd actually existed.

Diving For Bones

The next day, instead of my father, it was me sitting disconsolately in the shade of the Toad. I felt as though the heavy, inky dark of the drop-off was inside me. All around the air was full of the smell of sweet gale and cedar and the delicate rain-drop scent of fresh poplar leaves, but to me it all smelt like the ashes of the Burn. I couldn't help thinking about Eva and the look she'd had just before we started wrestling in the water – as though I weren't in the same world that she was seeing, not at all. It had been same with my father at the swamp house. No matter how close you were to someone, close enough to wrestle with them even, they could be in another place entirely. And you wouldn't ever know where and what that place was, or what you appeared like to them there – if you were apparent to them at all. And when they were in that place there might not be anything you could do, except wonder if there was something.

Eventually, I saw Oskar approaching along the trail. He had a shuffling maybe of a walk, like Chaplin playing shy. He sat down beside me, leaning his back on the Toad. I was glad he was okay but was so sunk in my misery I could barely say hello.

'Quite some catch the other day,' he said.

It'd been dark when we'd gotten back and I hadn't put the leeches in the pit beneath his cabin, which he called his cellar.

'I forgot.'

'You know, I never knew leeches got that big,' he said and I realised he was talking about Eva.

He took his baseball cap off, ran his hand down the back of his head, and then scrunched his eyes up against the glitter on the water as if it were a bag of spilt needles.

'You want to play some crib?' he asked.

Inside his cabin it was cramped and gloomy. An oil lamp sat extinguished on the card table. There were old newspapers taped over the single window, leftover from the winter, and above my head the teeth of some ancient metal traps grinned down from the cross-beams. In the far corner, beside a metal frame bed heaped with coarse, woollen Hudson's Bay blankets, was a pile of unsold muskrat hides. The whole place smelt of a mixture of fish scales and wood smoke and soot from the ugly black barrel stove that squatted in the corner opposite the bed. There was also a musky, sulphurous odour – a combination of rotten eggs and off meat, with a slight chemical reek underlying it – that must have come from the tanning solvents he'd used on the hides. The sweet gale and cedar seemed a long way away. In here it was as if the day itself had been skinned and tanned and turned inside out.

I tottered a few inches to the right as I approached the card table. The slant of the floor made it like the deck of a listing ship – it took a while to get your legs.

Oskar set our pegs in the holes he'd drilled into the table and began dealing.

'I'm sorry,' I blurted. 'I should've asked if I could take her. I wanted to show her where the prison was.'

Oskar finished dealing and cut the deck to see which one of us got the first crib.

'She likes old places and ruins. Or she likes taking pictures of them anyway.'

Oskar had already started playing. He put down a ten of diamonds and I put down a seven instead of my ten of clubs.

I was flustered and guilty. I didn't know what to say about the episode with Eva and the train. And I didn't know what to tell him about where we'd been and what had really happened. That we'd been on a wild goose chase? That we'd found the un-named water body and given it a name? That she'd been diving for bones?

'I don't know why she likes doing that,' I said. 'She does a lot of stuff I don't know the reasons for.'

Oskar played a seven and picked up a couple of points. Then I played a six and he got thirty-one with an ace and took another two points. Once we'd counted our hands he finally spoke.

'You know I don't trap out that way, don't you? That place has never been lucky. Bad luck is bad luck – there's no point getting too close to it if you don't need to.'

I didn't know how he knew we'd been up north of the prison site.

'She wanted to look there,' I said. 'I don't even know what she was expecting to find.'

'Sometimes people need to look for things they don't even want to find.'

After we'd finished a couple of games, Oskar walked across the room and pulled a bottle of Crown Royale out from beneath his bed and poured himself a glass. It was the first time I'd actually seen him drink. It was a piece of decorum he shared with many of the older drunks in town – not to drink in front of children or churches. He must have decided I was old enough now not to qualify.

'You want a glass?' he asked, sitting back down.

'Sure,' I said.

'Don't go telling your old man.'

'I won't.'

I'd never had alcohol before. I had a glass. He had the rest of the bottle.

But it was me who ended up the drunker.

'You said *never*,' I slurred after I'd finished my glass. I felt warm and cocooned. I felt like I could look at everything head on in the eye. 'You said it had *never* been lucky.'

'What had never been lucky?'

'*That place*,' I said emphatically, gesturing with my hands and accidently knocking one of my counters off the table. I was my father's son – perhaps it was inevitable I'd prove to be a clumsy drunk. '*Why never?*'

Oskar looked down at his knee for a second or two, as though he were consulting it on some grave issue.

'You remember what you asked me before?'

'It seems like I've been asking you a bunch of stuff lately,' I bellowed. The volume of my voice didn't feel entirely under my control.

'You asked if any of them escaped.'

'Any of who escaped?'

'The prisoners.'

His name wasn't Gunther. It was Johann. He was one of the prisoners Oskar played cards with. He remembered playing with them one particular night. It was the first week of November and they'd been there for almost a year. (Oskar said when they'd first arrived they'd talked to him about Christmas and how the war would be over and won by then and they'd be home. 'You'll be the one in here,' they'd joked. The second year they didn't talk or joke about it at all.) Outside a flurry of snow had fallen and then quickly melted. But by midnight it'd started turning cold fast. He'd noticed it on his hands and ears when he'd stepped outside for a cigarette. He'd started rubbing his palms together to keep them warm.

'Here, take these,' said Johann, who'd joined him outside for a smoke. He'd handed him a pair of black woollen gloves.

Once they were back inside they'd played for about another hour. Half way through a game of gin rummy Johann had thrown down his hand and stood abruptly up from the table.

'This is what we've done,' he'd said in English. 'Given up.' And then he'd turned and left.

'I didn't get a chance to give them back,' said Oskar.

By one in the morning it was cold enough for the puddles in the camp to have frozen over. Oskar remembered the sound of his boots crunching through them as he headed home. By the time he'd got back to his cabin there was a skin of ice covering a half drunk cup of coffee on his table.

The next morning began with a bright, hard frost. It took the sun a good few hours to clear it and in the shaded part of the woods it didn't clear at all. The lake was swathed in a heavy mist when he went back to the camp to return the gloves. It was giving up the very last dregs of the summer and fall's heat. Soon enough it'd be turning to ice.

But when he got there Johann was gone. Nobody had seen him since the night before. There weren't even any guards to notice he wasn't there; they were both drunk in town. The others prisoners weren't happy that he'd escaped. They were worried. It was already getting cold again and they knew enough about where they were to know the chances of him getting anywhere on foot were slim to zero. They spent most of the day out looking for him themselves and in the afternoon they found a small patch of blood beside some trees they'd been cutting for fuel.

At first no-one could work out what'd happened. Nobody had shot him – there hadn't been any guards. And there

133

wasn't even a fence or barbed wire to get over. It didn't make any sense. But it didn't take long to figure things out. Oskar just followed the blood trail. He'd obviously cut his leg or foot on a Swedish saw somebody had left leaning against a tree stump. It was dumb luck. And yet he'd kept on going.

Oskar said he didn't know why he'd agreed to track him. He guessed it was because he'd given him the gloves. It felt like he had a responsibility to find him somehow.

He'd blood-tracked him for a few hours, until it began to get dark.

'It was like going after a deer,' he said. 'Like that one from last year.

I began to suspect then that it hadn't ended well for Johann.

The previous fall Oskar had taken me deer hunting for the first time. We'd gone to an area east of the lake, where a logging company had clear-cut a patch of the forest two years before. The cut stretched jaggedly on either side of a rough winter road, which was corded with logs where it passed over the lowest, swampiest ground. Here and there the tops of small ridges had been left uncut, breaking up the slashed, brushy ground into a series of narrow, wooded islands. It had been a damp, cold morning, with flurries of sleet in the air, prefiguring the snow that had been promising for weeks but hadn't yet fallen. The whole landscape, as if in preparation for it, seemed to have been drained into a gaunt spectrum that ranged from wet black to grey. Even the green of the conifers looked grey.

We'd stood by the road to load our guns.

'I'll take the cut on this side of the road,' Oskar had said. 'And you take it on that side. Look for their tracks and their crap and what they eat. And when you're trying to spot them, don't go looking for a deer.'

The bafflement must have shown on my face.

'I mean, don't go looking for a deer just standing there square in the open. It doesn't happen that way too much. You probably won't even see the whole thing, not to start with anyways. Look for shapes and pieces first – an ear, or a tail, or a bit of antler.'

'And don't get lost,' he added, as he turned and started walking into the cut. He'd gone about ten feet before he turned back again.

'And don't shoot me neither,' he said.

I'd gone about half a mile when I saw an eye. It was at the very edge of the cut and it'd probably been looking at me for a while before I started looking at it. And once I'd seen the eye the rest of it sort of just slowly materialised into a deer, like I was putting together a jigsaw made of mist. My hands were trembling and I didn't breathe right and when I shot it disappeared. It was as though it'd never been there, as though I'd fired at a ghost. I waited until eventually Oskar appeared. I told him what'd happened.

'Where was it?' he asked. 'When you shot?'

Without the deer there the bush looked all the same.

'Over there, I think,' I said. 'I think I missed him. I'm pretty sure I missed him.'

'We'll see,' said Oskar.

For half an hour we looked. And then, a long way from where I thought it had been, lost in that tangled ocean of grey, Oskar found a speck of blood.

'You wounded him,' he said.

And all the excitement I'd felt that morning had suddenly turned into an awful, sick heaviness that sank onto the bottom of my stomach.

'What do we do?' I croaked.

'We find him,' Oskar said.

135

It took Oskar an hour to track it, with me following forlornly in his wake. Every few hundred yards he'd turn up some new evidence of how badly I'd shot. He began finding splinters of bone as well as blood.

'You hit him in the leg,' he said. I wished I'd never pulled the trigger.

Eventually, we found it in a swale between a wooded ridge and a beaver pond. It was too weak to run any further on its three good legs. Oskar finished it with a single shot and it fell on the grass. When we got up close I could see its tongue lolling out of its mouth and the steam coming off its hide, like a final exhalation of breath, and it was as though I'd swallowed every ounce of grey in the world and I slumped down miserably onto the grass beside it.

Oskar handed me his knife.

'Now you got to gut it,' he said. 'And next time don't shoot if you don't think you're going to kill it clean.'

Oskar said he'd gone back first thing the next morning and found the prisoner within a couple of hours.

'How far did he get?' I asked.

'About ten miles,' he said.

'And where did you find him?'

He said he'd followed the bank of the same creek Eva and I must have taken in his boat. And where the creek had begun to get shallow and rocky the trail had switched into the woods. Oskar said he'd eventually come to a small lake and that was where he'd found him. He was sitting on the shoreline, facing the east like some poet or dreamer waiting for the sunrise. The cut from the saw wasn't so bad, Oskar said. It was the cold that'd killed him. He must have been waiting for the sun to come up and warm him. And there it was, sewn right onto the back of his prisoner jacket: that big

136

red circle, as if the sun had played a trick and snuck up behind him instead.

'But I still gave them back,' Oskar said.

'Gave what back?'

'His gloves,' he said. 'I put them back on his hands right there and then, before I started dragging him back to the camp.'

Outside Oskar's cabin the day had moved on more quickly than I'd thought. On my walk home I discovered the shadow beneath the Toad had shifted right around. Across the bay the trees on the islands were beginning to turn that rich and vivid green the falling sun brings out. And whether it was the whiskey or the elapsed time or even, oddly, the sadness of Oskar's story, I found my spirits not quite so low as before. It was like the deer, I thought: you only ever saw shapes and pieces – even of people – and it was pointless worrying about ever seeing the whole thing.

At dinner that evening I tried to stay as quiet as possible. I wasn't sure whether I'd have control of the volume of my voice back again and I didn't want my father to know I'd been drinking. Not that there was a huge risk of my voice betraying me. We were dealing mainly in single words and phrases. 'It'll be a beautiful sunset,' my father had said twice, before stumbling to an awkward halt. We hadn't really spoken to each other properly since the trip to the swamp house. The meatloaf on the table and the skin on my father's face looked a similar colour to the world the morning I'd shot my deer: a kind of universal grey.

Both of us kept looking hopefully out the window. My father tried to pull a piece of curtain aside and the rail came down. But it was too late. Mrs Schneider wasn't swimming. Neither was Judith.

My father spent several minutes shifting cutlery vigorously back and forth from one side of his plate to the other. At one point he leapt up to tidy away the fallen curtain rail and ended up polishing a non-existent smudge on the glass of the window, all the while glancing forlornly out of it as if he hadn't quite given up on spotting an arm or a leg breaking the surface of the water. The sun had turned its first shade of red and the colour seemed to bounce off the lake and up into his grey cheeks.

'We don't have to keep going back there,' he suddenly blurted.

I nodded. We'd only gone there one time since we'd moved but that didn't seem important.

'She wouldn't mind.'

I nodded again.

The skin on his face seemed to have become several shades redder. And I was glad. It was good to see the blood back in them. He tucked decisively into his meatloaf as if a great weight had been lifted from him.

After he'd finished eating he said, 'You know, Mrs Schneider's snap peas are getting pretty high.'

We looked out towards her back garden. He was right. They were.

'They are,' I said.

'We don't have to,' he repeated.

As I was finishing my own meatloaf he looked out at the lake. 'It is a beautiful sunset,' he said. 'Isn't it something,' he said, turning towards me and breaking out into a wide and unexpected smile.

'And I bethought me of the playful Hare,' he said.

'Hare?' I said.

'From the leech poem,' he said.

I wasn't entirely sure what a hare might have to do with

138

anything. But it was good to see him this way, with the reddening light warming his cheeks and colouring the lenses of his glasses. Outside the sky really was quite something. It was beautiful, as he'd said it was. But I wasn't really looking at it. All I could look at was the key to the truck that was hanging from the gun rack. The sun had almost set and I'd come to pretty much the very opposite conclusion my father had.

Shapes and Pieces

It seemed to take a great age for the sun to finally go down, and then another one for my father to put aside his book (which was about ancient pottery, I was glad to see) and go to bed. I waited until the sound of his nightly struggles with his slightly too short bed-frame subsided before heading out.

Because there was no official crossing, my father had always parked our truck on the other side of the tracks, in a space he'd cleared at the side of the logging road. As I was crossing I caught side of the tell-tale glow from one of Eva's cigarettes. It was over by the culvert and without thinking I began walking towards it. About fifty or so yards away I spotted another light through a gap in the trees. This was different. It came from a small flame.

At first I thought it must be from a campfire but it was a single flame – there were no others. A closer look revealed it to be from a lamp. In the small, wavering circle of its light, I could make out the figure of Lamar. He was still hammering away at his new building. The flame from the lamp illuminated his neck and face from below, making him look like a blacksmith at his forge. The moths were flickering so thickly around the circle of light it was as if he was working in a snowstorm. Eva must have been watching him from among the bulrushes.

I took a few strides further and then stopped. A feeling had come upon me that none of the signs Lamar had put up around his property had ever once inspired: a feeling of trespass. It felt as though I'd stumbled upon some mysterious rite or ritual, I had no place being.

In comparison to the light of the cigarette and the lamp, the headlights of the truck looked huge and monstrous. It felt as though the entire lake must have been lit up by them. It seemed impossible they wouldn't rush directly towards my father's bedroom window, crashing through it in a blinding flash and waking him instantly. It was only after I'd managed to get a good kilometre down the logging road that my heartbeat began to slow.

I'd never driven at night. In fact, I'd never driven by myself before because I didn't have a licence yet. I'd never stolen my father's truck before, for that matter. To begin with it was all I could do to work out the high and low beams and get used to the empty seat next to me. Everything appeared exaggerated – the distances, my speed, the darkness of the night, the brightness of the headlights. Even the tiny clicking of the moths and bugs hitting the windscreen sounded as loud as hail. I concentrated so intently on the visible strip of road in front of me, and went so slowly, it was as if I was creeping along a tunnel on my hands and knees. But, by the time I'd reached the highway, I'd relaxed enough to begin looking about me.

Apart from a couple of logging trucks which thundered past, lit up like mobile villages, nobody else was on the road. The lines slipped by beneath me and I started searching the edges and ditches for the reflected eyes of animals. This had always been a favourite game of ours when we'd driven at night. It had been a great thrill to spot a pair of them, call out your first guess of what it might be, and then see if you were right. Except part of the thrill of this game, I now remembered, had been the ones you passed by without ever quite knowing. They could be anything you wanted.

I was beginning to enjoy driving by myself – there was something soothing, lulling even, about the sleek, black, curving emptiness of the tarmac, about the lines slipping by – when all too soon I'd arrived. I'd almost forgotten what it was I was going there to do.

It was different at night. The moment I stepped out of the truck I could hear frogs calling. The leaves of the saplings on the track rustled as I brushed past them. Somewhere nearby a loon was keening. It was noisy out. The dark was full of sound.

For a brief moment it was as though the night had pushed back the swamp. Its surface was nearly invisible. You could only make out the vague shapes of the trees, with their gaunt trunks and pale twiggy fingers. But, gradually, what little light there was from the sliver of the moon, revealed it. I was standing right at its edge. The house was below my feet, its outline dimly reflected in the coldly still and slick surface of the water. I could smell the lilacs my father had planted. I could see the space where he'd taken down the bathroom; my eyes seemed to probe involuntarily at its absence like a tongue at the gum beneath a missing tooth.

It wasn't until I'd taken my initial steps into the water that it even occurred to me to be frightened or disturbed. But once I had taken them it was awful. The bottom of the swamp wasn't solid; my feet plunged through rotting twigs and branches and the sludge of shed leaves and every slippery dead thing I could imagine. Putting my hand down into it was even worse.

The first thing I found was the blanket. The cribbage board was further out. The water was almost up to my thighs and I had to reach my arm in right up to my shoulder to seek it out with my fingers. It was while I was searching for the pancake griddle that I discovered the first of my mother's sculptures.

To begin with I didn't know what it was and it says something about what was down there on the bottom of the swamp that it was a sort of relief when I realised my fingers were brushing against bone. The first thing I recognised were the whittling marks: the moment I felt them I knew exactly what they were and who had made them. I carried the sculpture back to the shore, placed it on the blanket, and immediately waded out in search of another one.

How long I waded through that swamp I couldn't say for sure, but in the end I must have looked like Eva had looked at Hummingbird Lake – and smelt far worse. What my fingers touched that night I don't fully know and wouldn't want to say. All I do know is that once I'd tired myself out there were four of my mother's sculptures sitting on the wet blanket and I was slumped next to them like an exhausted head-hunter beside his trophies. I never recovered the pancake griddle.

It had been many years since I'd seen one of these sculptures, or even consciously thought of them, though in other ways they had always been there; staring at me from the edges of my thoughts – a pair of luminous and enigmatic eyes. Perhaps this accounted for the strange mixture of familiarity and bewilderment they inspired in me. As I said, I recognised each indentation, each chiselled curve, but at the same time I couldn't tell which one was which; for instance, I had no clear memory of what wall they'd hung on, or what table they'd sat on, let alone of what they'd been meant to be.

For a long time I just sat there, picking them up one by one and running my hands over them. It was as though I'd forgotten where I was and what time it was and how I'd got there – all that had become suspended somewhere at the very back of my mind. And then it all began to come rushing back

143

and it was intensified somehow, as though an invisible dial had been turned up. I was cold and shivery. The smell of the lilacs was so thick and heavy it was choking me. The sound of the frogs was loud, much too loud, until it was taut and bulged like the skin of their throats.

The whole night was swelling with it as I wrapped the sculptures in the blanket

I don't really remember driving back. I only remember being aware the whole time of the bulging presence of the blanket on the seat beside me. It felt as though I was sitting next to a wriggling sack – precariously fastened and filled with some unknown animal or animals. When I got back to my room I put the cribbage board and the blanket and the sculptures in the dresser at the end of my bed. After a few sleepless hours I draped my spare blankets over the dresser. An hour later I wrapped the sleeping bag I used for camping around it. Then the blankets and sheets I was lying under. Then my winter coat and clothes.

And still I couldn't sleep.

Lighthouses

'Hello, ground control to Zachary Taylor,' Eva said.

She was sitting on her bed, beside the window. I was staring at the photographs on her wall. I couldn't stop staring. It was the type of hot, humid, fly-papery afternoon when your attention seems to catch and stick on the surface of things. It had been a long night and half the day had already been gone when I'd woken.

On the walk over to Butterfly Creek the air – rising up from the sun-baked cinders and chippings, from the long ribbons of rail – had wobbled and appeared (if air can do such a thing) to sweat. Even the sounds of the cicadas and crickets had been slurry and indefinite, sliding on notes that seemed to extend further and longer than they should, like somebody slowly rubbing the strings of a guitar with their finger. Along the verges the orange and yellow hawkweed had glowed like a thousand tiny heating lamps.

There was one photograph in particular my attention kept catching on. It was of an abandoned summer camp somewhere in the south of the province. At first glance you might not have noticed it was abandoned at all; it showed a clearing at the edge of a lake surrounded by maples, amongst which nestled six neat, square cabins. A wooden dock protruded out into the water and behind it on the shore was a small field that had probably been used for sports of one type or another. If you looked very closely you could just about make out a baseball bat, flung carelessly into the grass beyond a possible first base. There were still clotheslines hanging between the trees outside the cabins, waiting for towels and bathing suits. It would have been easy to imagine the whole place was simply awaiting the arrival of the children and counsellors for the summer, or for them to return from some group excursion. But that closer look also revealed several unmistakable signs of dereliction. The grass had grown high above the dry earth, once pounded smooth and bare by running shoes and heels. Saplings had taken root. The dock had been twisted and splintered by the winter ice; while beside it, on a narrow strip of sand, were the ribs of a mouldering canoe. The cheery red paint on the door and window frames had faded to a dull orange and was flaking like rust.

'Jesus,' Eva said, getting up and standing between me and the wall, 'where have you been?'

'I was just looking at them,' I said.

'You're always just *looking* at stuff,' she said impatiently. 'And you don't *see* anything.'

'What do you mean?' I said. 'Like what?'

'Like that,' she said, turning and pointing out the window.

Outside, Lamar was hammering some boards onto the frame he'd been building earlier, the one I'd thought had been a new no trespassing sign. I'd walked past him on my way in. We'd nodded at each other and then I'd carefully examined the ground and he'd started looking for some suddenly crucial thing in his nail bucket.

'You know what he's building, don't you?'

I didn't know. I was used to minding my own business where Lamar was concerned. It was the polite thing to do for people who preferred to be left alone.

'A new outhouse?'

146

Eva looked at me as though I'd just announced the world was triangular.

'It's a lighthouse.'

I looked at her the same way.

'A lighthouse,' I said, and then couldn't think of anything else to add. 'It's a bit small for a lighthouse.'

'Jesus H Christ, Zachary. He can hardly build one the exact same size, can he?'

I glanced back out the open window. Waves of heat were wobbling up and down along the banks of the creek, creating a shimmery illusion of movement. The bow of Lamar's boat seemed to rise and fall on the water, as though it were bobbing in a sea swell. From the surrounding reeds and rushes came the darkly wet, slightly fishy, smell of a swamp. Lamar continued to hammer away, apparently oblivious to the swarm of deerflies that was orbiting madly around his head like a solar system whose physics had gone kaput.

'The same size as what?' I finally asked.

'As the one in his pictures, dummy.'

We walked out into the main room. Once I knew what I was looking for I saw it pretty quickly. The boat I recognised instantly. It was moored on a small quay beside some grey timbered fish sheds. You could see it to the left of the shark. Of course, it couldn't have been the exact same boat, but it was the exact same kind of boat. Even the colours were the same.

'And the car,' Eva prompted.

I looked at another of the photographs, the one with the family standing beside their car. Yes, I could see that too now: the car was a blue Oldsmobile. On the opposite wall the animals stared blankly ahead with their shiny eyes, as though caught in its headlights.

147

'And the lighthouse.'

That was more difficult. In the photographs a tall, white tower sat on a slab of bare rock, topped by a red lantern room and roof. Whatever Lamar was building he had a long way to go, even to create it in miniature. But the basic shape was there. There was no mistaking it.

'Can you see now?' Eva said.

When we were back in her room, Eva told me all of the photographs were from the holiday they'd gone on the year before her parents had died. They'd spent a week at Peggy's Cove in Nova Scotia.

'Ever since I came to stay here it's all he talks about,' she said. 'And the way he talks about it you'd think it was last year we went, or last week, and we were all planning on going back.'

She told me it was the same as any holiday you went on as a kid: some things stood out, others weren't that clear; big chunks were just forgotten. She remembered the shark and the lighthouse and the boat trip and the sea. But her uncle remembered everything.

'One day he started going on about a hat my mom had worn on a beach down the coast, and how a breeze had blown it off. It was twenty-one degrees out and the breeze was a gentle easterly, he says. I mean, who remembers shit like that!'

As she spoke, Eva moved over to her bed and sat on it. She drew her knees up in front of her and started rubbing the bare patch beneath her ear so hard I was worried the skin might break and bleed again. Through the window I could hear the thunk thunk thunk of Lamar's hammer.

'I don't know. To him it was like this perfect trip and everything needed to be witnessed and noted like it was important, like he might be putting it into a book in the bible. So that day on the boat: I remember him and my dad catching some cod and mackerel and that in the evening we ate lobsters in a restaurant. But my uncle remembers exactly how many fish were caught. He remembers which frigging table we sat at. He remembers the waitress was wearing a blue and white check apron.'

'And then all those photos on the wall,' Eva said. 'And the boat, and the car. And now that fucking lighthouse. It's weird.'

It was, I thought. But a lot of stuff could seem that way. Eva's hair and clothes could seem weird. My father's explorer quotes could seem weird. Oskar's skulls could. It could all seem weird if you only saw the shapes and pieces. A deer could look like a unicorn if you only saw the tip of its antler. I was feeling quite philosophical after my day with Oskar and sitting under the Toad.

'Maybe he wants to remember it because of what happened afterwards,' I said thoughtfully. 'And those things are just a way to help him.'

Eva had got up from the bed.

'Oh, and who's the big thinker now.'

'I'm just saying…'

'You're just saying shit…'

Her 's's had begun to slur as though she were suddenly drunk. She'd started pacing back and forth in front of the window and her eyes had that same glazed and quizzical expression they'd had at the un-named water body. It was like the way you could sometimes sense the weather was about to shift from looking at the surface of the lake.

'Jesus H frigging fucking Christ!' she spat out. 'Oh, it was so perfect and the waitress was wearing a blue and white check apron and your mother said the lobster's eyes were scary and everyone was making a joke about what you could see see see …'

I knew she wasn't speaking to me anymore. I doubted I was even really there. Instinctively, I tried to get myself between her and the window.

'But it wasn't all happy like that. He remembers nothing. He remembers jack shit.'

I managed to slide myself onto the sill. Outside, beyond the thunk thunking of the hammer, I could hear the slow chirrup of crickets in the humid air. They had the same wet, slurry edges as Eva's 's's.

'I remember exactly how I felt in that restaurant,' she said. 'I was bored and I was as pissed as vinegar. My parents had been fighting the whole time we'd been getting ready to go to the place. My mom had been saying why do we have to go everywhere with Lamar? Why can't we have a family holiday on our own just once? And my dad was saying what was the big deal, we always went with Lamar. He was our family too. And my mom was saying that wasn't the point, not at all, and that next year we changed things. And dad was saying but next year was already arranged. And mom was saying the year after that then. Just one frigging holiday, she said. It'd be good for us and it wasn't going to kill him. And then we were in the restaurant putting on our smiles for Lamar and the waitress and everybody else and his lobster, and making fucking jokes about the see see SEE …'

The first two sees were slurred right into my face. The final one was shouted out of the window. It seemed to combine with the cricket song, as though it were an amplification of it. Lamar put down his hammer. Eva shoved past me and leant out the window.

'It wasn't like that,' she shouted.

150

We were just close enough to see Lamar's eyebrows begin to twitch.

'It wasn't like that,' she repeated. 'It wasn't. Just like that fucking boat isn't the fucking boat and that lighthouse isn't a fucking lighthouse and those fish and animals on your walls aren't fish and fucking animals!'

By now Eva was leaning halfway out of the window and Lamar's eyebrows were writhing on his forehead.

'You know what,' she shouted. 'They didn't even *want* you there. Did you know that? They didn't even *want* you there!' Then she paused, as if gathering extra breath.

'If it wasn't for you and your perfect fucking holidays they'd be alive,' she shouted. 'Have you ever thought about that, Lamar? Have you ever thought about THAT!'

Lamar didn't say anything. He just bowed his head and stared at the ground.

I don't remember leaving Butterfly Creek that day. What I do remember is that I didn't go straight home. Instead, I followed the tracks out towards Wannigan Bay. I guess I'd wanted to try to lose myself in the still quiet of the underwater; to watch the pike hover at the edge of the weeds and forget everything else. But I never arrived there. All I could think about as I walked was the photograph of the summer camp and that brief moment when I'd first looked at it and thought maybe I'd been wrong about it being another of Eva's ruins; that maybe a bunch of canoes laden with singing children was about to pull up to the dock and the field fill with bare feet and the bat to knock a ball out into centre field. But it was only the photograph's trick – to create that moment, that merest second of suspension; a poised fraction of time and space where everything was possible and nothing had happened yet; where portents and signs and omens could mean anything, even their opposite; where a door could be closed if you wanted it to be closed; or if it was ajar and you'd slipped away from the police officer's grasp to look through it, then what you saw could mean something else entirely: there it would all be – a cigarette butt in the ashtray, the mirror fogged with steam, the scent of soap and perfume in the air – and the person who left them, the person who was staring at you with the too still and too big eyes, would be able to see you and would be able to hear what you shouted out to them and would be always and forever about to lift themselves out from the water.

And then I sat down beside the tracks and wept.

Gardens

When I finally did get back home I found my father helping Judith in her mother's vegetable garden. It wasn't something I was expecting to find and so I paused for a while, out of sight behind a red pine. I wasn't sure what I thought about this. Mrs Schneider was nowhere to be seen.

My father was tying lines of string onto bamboo poles for the snap peas to grow onto. They'd already grown almost unfeasibly high and he needed his full reach to get above them.

It was the same with the rest of Mrs Schneider's garden. Everything bulged and sprouted and swelled in remarkable proportions and abundance. Here, on the thin, meagre soil of the shield, there was a hint of the miraculous about it; and for me, the scion of failed farmers, this garden had always been something of a marvel. Mrs Schneider had the greenest thumb I knew and seeing her daughter in her garden I couldn't help imagining her as the product of this same fructifying touch. I began looking at her in the same way you might an unusually large squash or carrot.

My father, after his first efforts at the swamp house, hadn't been near a seed, let alone a garden. But he appeared comfortable enough in this one. He was wearing a green bug hat and his face was half hidden behind its mesh. As he fumbled with the strings for the snap peas he looked like a huge stick insect standing on its back legs and trying to roll a cigarette. His voice, coming through the mesh, was just audible from where I stood.

He was telling Judith about the 1858 Cayley-Galt tariff act. Somewhat to my astonishment, she asked a question about it.

I loitered a few more minutes and realised that what I was thinking was that it was okay. It was fine. When I stepped out from behind the red pine they both greeted me with loud, overly effusive voices.

We all stood awkwardly in the shadow of the snap peas for a second or two before my father started tying and retying their strings and Judith began showing me everything in the garden as though it were a species of exotic flora. Look, she'd say, see how the chard's coming up nicely here. Isn't the spinach doing great? See, the tomatoes should be good this year. After she'd finished showing me everything she stood up straight and pushed back her shoulders.

The sun was dipping down towards the edge of the second island and as the light faded the noise of mosquitoes began swelling. At this time of the year my father and I didn't eat supper at any set hour; we'd usually just wait until both of us were hungry. (My father didn't see the need for routines if they weren't connected to anything. Outside of the school year we lived pretty much like college students.) So I was surprised when he suddenly announced it was our supper time. He announced it … and then stood exactly where he was, as if his feet were set in cement. The stalks of several snap peas fell away from the string.

After about a minute Judith said, 'You should have some of these. For your supper,' and started frantically picking unready leaves of chard and spinach. Some of them were only a few inches high.

My father spent a long time standing exactly where he was, and Judith had destroyed a good portion of her mother's greens, before he finally said, 'Why don't you join us?' Hastily adding '…and your mother too.'

'Thank you. I'd love to,' Judith said. She didn't mention her mother.

After we'd eaten on the porch my father went into the kitchen to make coffee and started worrying about our cups. I knew he was worrying about them because I could hear him banging crockery as he looked for others, which he knew as well as I did we didn't have. Most of the crockery – like most of the stuff in the cabin – we'd inherited from my grandfather (or rather we'd kept it pretty much as he'd left it). My grandfather had been a keen sportsman and so a great number of our household goods and decorations were themed around fish and game, which delighted me but which my father must have just that second realised he felt slightly embarrassed about (especially considering that Judith was a biologist). There were prints of grouse and pheasants on the walls. An illustrated woodcut of the fisherman's prayer sat on the wall by the door, beside the empty gun rack. A yellow plaque engraved with 'Biggest Lake Trout 1937' took pride of place over the stone fireplace. Every one of our cups was illustrated with a different species of duck.

My father, figuring on safety in numbers, brought a selection in with the coffee pot.

'Any preference?' he asked.

'I'll have a mallard,' Judith said. 'I'm just a simple girl – none of your fancy ducks for me.'

My father broke out into his goofy, lopsided smile and I excused myself, saying I was going out to hunt for toads.

I hadn't really gone out toad hunting for about five years. As a child it'd been one of my favourite pursuits. As soon as it was dark I'd head out and collect as many as I could in a

155

bucket and then release them outside our cabin. I'd been told they protected us from the bugs.

The day was long gone and there was no moon and outside, beyond the light that spilled out from the porch windows, everything was dark. As I shuffled through it towards the dock I was amazed at how nonchalantly I'd once scoured this shore, alone, with only a flashlight and my bucket. I'd not been afraid of the night back then, though now I often felt unsettled by it, as though it were full of spirits of one sort or another – good and bad both.

A light flared on the end of the dock. For a second my heart began to jump and I stepped quickly back into the illuminated space in front of the cabin. But then the light settled into a small orange disc and I could smell the acrid, and now familiar, scent of a green death.

'Nothing to see out here,' Eva said. She must have been watching me since I'd come out the door. I didn't know how long she'd been standing on our dock.

I watched as the cigarette end bobbed its way to the edge of the spilled light, until I could make out the pale oval of her face. Her black wig merged into the darkness behind, making it look as though it were a vast cowl. Her eyes were shiny, like those of wild animals caught by headlights on the sides of highways.

'I see you gentlemen have lured a lady into your abode,' she said quietly in her southern accent.

'That's Judith,' I whispered. 'She's Mrs Schneider's daughter. She's divorced.'

'Jesus, Zachary, I know who it is. We're in Sitting Down Lake; population: seven. She'd be kind of hard to miss, don't you think.'

Without saying anything more we moved further down the shoreline. Away from the light you could barely see a few inches in front of your nose. I followed the tip of Eva's cigarette. When we stopped I turned around and the windows of the porch were like a film screen in a dark cinema or one of those guy's paintings where you're looking into rooms from the outside. Judith was looking at the other cups. My father's elbows were propped on the table where they couldn't do any damage. He was laughing.

It was easier to ask Eva things now I couldn't see her face. I could hear the low, banjo thrum of green frogs. The air was humming with invisible insects.

'What happened with Lamar?' I asked.

'He never said anything. He went and sat in the cabin of his boat,' Eva said. 'Actually, he's still sitting in the cabin of his boat. If he could, I think he'd sail it the hell out of Dodge. I shouldn't have said all that stuff.'

'You can stay here with us,' I said. 'If you don't want to go back.'

'It's okay,' she said. 'He's okay, you know. He's weird but he's not dangerous weird or anything. He was being weird in a kind sort of way, if that makes sense. All that lighthouse and car and boat shit, he did it for me. I think he honestly thought it'd be good for me – for the both of us. That it'd take us back to happier times. And you know what? Whatever Lamar is, he's all I've really got.'

And then we stood there for a while, silently, as though our voices had been gulped down by the frogs and toads.

'I watched you guys eating,' Eva finally said.

'It was nice,' she said. I thought she might be joking or being sarcastic but she wasn't. Her voice was sad, like I'd never heard it be before.

'It was really nice,' she said.

The New Burn

I woke up late in the morning to the smell of smoke. At first I thought my father must have lit a fire but the night had been a warm one, so warm I'd kicked off my blankets and drenched my pillow with sweat. And then I thought of forest fires and Mrs Molson's house and the cruel, cinder-black finger of the burn and found that my limbs were momentarily useless, as if I'd not woken properly at all and was still half-caught in the paralysis of a dream.

'Zachary,' a voice called from outside my window. 'Zachary, you better get up.' It was my father's voice.

When I did manage to get up I found him outside the porch in his old-fashioned night gown (he was the only man I can ever remember wearing one), pacing up and down the shore and sniffing the air. He looked like an illustration of Scrooge arguing with his ghosts. Every few yards he'd stop and stamp the ground angrily with his foot, as though the smoke were his fault. I think by then he'd come to see calamity as directly correlated to his own happiness; that the moment he actually felt some it would strike. I think he thought he had brought a forest fire down upon us.

Before going to bed I'd read his book of quotations and found an excerpt from Thomson newly written there. It was different from the others. It was about winter (and not about how it froze your supplies or killed your sled dogs or gave you frostbite).

'A curious formation now takes place called Rime, of extreme thinness, adhering to the trees, willows and everything it can fasten on, it's beautiful, clear, spangles forming flowers of every shape, of a most brilliant appearance, and the sun shining on them makes them too dazzling to the sight. The lower the ground, the larger is the leaf, and the flower; this brilliant Rime can only be formed in calm clear weather and a gale of wind sweeps away all this magic scenery, to be reformed on calm days; it appears to be formed of frozen dew.'

My father made me stand on the end of the dock as he sniffed and stomped. As it turned out, I had a much clearer view of what was happening. There was no tell-tale haze on the horizon, or any other sign of a forest fire. The smoke was spiralling up in single columns and had only one origin.

'It's Butterfly Creek,' I shouted.

At first my father didn't want me to go but there was no stopping me and so he relented and we approached Butterfly Creek together by way of the tracks.

Mrs Schneider and Judith were already standing by the culvert.

'All of it,' Mrs Schneider exclaimed, gesturing towards Lamar's place with a single upturned palm.

'It doesn't look good, John,' Judith said to my father.

It didn't. From the culvert, through the cattails, you could see the deck of the boat had become a floating cradle of flames, like a ship in a Viking funeral. Its double shimmered beneath it, gently rocking in the serene, almost un-rippled, water of the creek.

The fire had worked quickly. The unfinished lighthouse tower was already a circle of smouldering ash; while beyond it the flames were rising up out of the collapsing roof of the main cabin. The still, morning air was heavy with the scent of burning pine and another, more acrid smell, that even from a distance stung the back of my throat. Almost as an afterthought I glanced over towards where the Oldsmobile had been parked: a thick, black smoke was billowing out from its broken windows.

'Did you see them?' my father asked.

'All of it,' Mrs Schneider repeated.

'I don't know,' Judith said, flustered. 'We just got here. We haven't seen anyone. I don't think we saw anyone.'

'Nobody?'

'No, nobody.'

Before I knew it my father was up to his thighs in the cattails and goose shit, wading down the creek towards the cabin. And I was following him.

We'd gone no more than a few feet before he noticed me.

'Go back,' he said, wheeling around and almost losing his balance and falling.

I stood exactly where I was, like a dog pretending not to hear a command. My father took several deep breaths and tried to sound calm and reasonable.

'You can't come, Zack, it's not safe. Go back to the tracks.'

I didn't move an inch. I wasn't going to leave him.

He looked over at the cabin and then at me several times in quick succession. 'Go back,' he said, all his forced composure gone. 'Go back,' he kept saying, flapping his arms awkwardly from side to side. He looked like an outraged heron.

How long we might have stayed fixed in these positions, I don't know. We'd been in them for at least a minute or two when we realised Judith was shouting at us. 'There's somebody coming,' she was shouting, pointing down the tracks.

They'd already rounded the bend and passed the burn by the time we'd got back up onto the tracks. My father and Judith squinted to see who it was. Mrs Schneider was still transfixed by the fire and hardly turned her head. I only needed to see the shuffling slightly sideways footsteps to know.

'It's Oskar,' I told them.

'There's nobody in there,' he said as soon as he reached us, as though he'd known what our first question would be.

'Are you sure?' my father asked.

'As sure as I'm standing here I'm sure.'

My father and Judith looked less reassured than they might have been. Oskar didn't appear one hundred per cent sure of where he was standing. His eyes were badly bloodshot and his hands and legs were shaking. You could smell the whiskey over the smoke.

'Where are they, Oskar?' Judith asked.

'Now that I can't be sure of. But I can tell you for certain they're not in those buildings or on that boat.'

'But…' my father began. He'd obviously been about to ask Oskar how he was certain but had stopped himself. He must have been thinking what I was thinking: that Oskar had seen something happen; that he'd been somewhere close by after one of his nature sleeps; that it would be rude and unkind to make him explain this.

Oskar shuffled over to stand beside Mrs Schneider and together they stared at the fire. As he'd got closer I'd seen Mrs Schneider subtly stiffen and straighten her back. It was her usual reaction to him and what she referred to – if she referred to them at all – as 'his difficulties.' She'd had many decades to master the polite and tolerant disapproval that allows small places to function. I'm not sure if Oskar had ever noticed it, or if he secretly enjoyed provoking it. They stood there together for some time before we left. Mrs Schneider looking

161

like she was watching the cities of the plain burn; Oskar looking like he'd just come from them.

There was a phone nailed to one of the electricity poles near where the station house had been. You could, in theory, use it to make emergency calls. Nobody had tried using it in several years. When my father picked up the receiver to phone the fire station and police the cord broke.

'I guess I better drive in,' he said, still holding the receiver in his hand, the snapped cord dangling beneath it. 'You should come with me,' he said, waving the receiver and its cord in front of us.

'I'm not going anywhere,' Mrs Schneider said, backing away from the cord.

'It's fine, John,' Judith said. 'It's not spreading. We'll be fine here.'

He told me to keep away from the fire. He told everybody to stay away from the fire and then got into his truck and drove off. Judith and Mrs Schneider walked back to their cabin. Two minutes later I heard the truck on the road and my father reappeared.

'You should come,' he said.

'I'm safe,' I said. 'I'll be safe.'

'Stay away from the fire,' he said.

As soon as he was out of sight I turned around and walked straight back down the tracks. Oskar was still there, sitting on a fallen tree near the culvert. I sat down beside him and together we watched Lamar's place burn.

Tablecloths

'It was him that burnt it,' Oskar said. One of the walls of the cabin had just fallen inwards and a cloud of sparks was rushing up into the sky. On the creek the boat continued to burn, but the flames had become patchy and intermittent. Despite everything it was still afloat.

As it turned out, my father and I had been right: Oskar had seen what'd happened. He'd woken up a few yards from where we were now sitting, he told me.

'I knew something was odd the moment I opened my eyes,' he said.

He said someone had put a table out on the grass in front of the cabin. Except it wasn't just a table. He'd rubbed his eyes and sat up and made sure he really was awake before he'd taken a second look. The table was perfectly set. There were knives and forks and plates and glasses and a tablecloth. There was a candle holder. It looked like something from a restaurant, Oskar told me. It was six o' clock in morning. The sun had only just come up.

It was Eva he'd seen first. She'd come out the front door holding a jug and put it on the table. Then she'd poured water into the glasses from the jug. Then she'd gone back to the cabin and started throwing pebbles up at Lamar's bedroom window.

He was going to leave then, Oskar said. He didn't want to be a snoop. But there were too many odd things happening. And he didn't want to go until he knew all this was an okay kind of odd and not a dangerous kind. He

163

didn't want to go until he knew she was going to be okay; her and Lamar both.

For instance, he told me, she'd been dressed funny; in one of those tee-shirts kids wear – with a superhero on it. Spiderman or one of those, he hadn't been sure. And it was way too small for her. The sleeves had barely come past her elbows.

After she'd thrown the pebbles Eva had walked over to the table and sat down on one of the two chairs, the one facing the cabin. She was smiling the whole time. Oskar said that when Lamar opened that front door and saw what was waiting for him it looked like his forehead was going to escape from his face and run off into the bush.

'What colour was it?' I asked.

Oskar looked at me, confused. 'What colour was what?'

'What colour was the tablecloth?'

'The tablecloth?'

'The tablecloth.'

'I don't know. It was blue maybe. I think it was blue.'

Lamar had stood there in the doorway for a good minute or two. And all the while Eva had continued smiling. 'Like a simple person's smile,' Oskar said. She'd gestured to Lamar to come over and sit at the table. Eventually, he'd walked over – slowly, very slowly. Before sitting down he'd held the chair tightly and pressed it against the ground as though he suspected it might be a trick one.

And then they'd sat there, facing each other across the table, as though they were having dinner in a restaurant, while the mist from the creek drifted over them and the beams of the newly risen sun split through it and glinted orange and golden on the water and lit up the trees. A couple of ducks flew right over their heads. Squirrels chided them from the edge of the woods. Silently, a raven settled in the topmost boughs of a pine.

After a few minutes they started speaking. Or rather, as far as Oskar could tell, it was mostly Eva speaking and Lamar nodding his head up and down, looking at her and not looking at her at the same time, as though he'd injured some part of himself and was afraid to examine it too closely. But despite the stillness of the morning Oskar couldn't hear what she was saying. Not while she was speaking in normal tones.

And then her smile had finally broken and her voice had escaped out through the debris. It got louder and louder, until Oskar could hear it. 'But it's okay,' Eva was saying. 'We can do this. We can eat together. We can pretend like we're there, Lamar. It can be like it was if you want it to be. I don't mind. It can be like it was. It's okay.'

Lamar's head was nodding and his mouth was open. His lips seemed to be moving but Oskar couldn't hear what he saying, if he was actually saying anything at all. His face was making it pretty clear that this wasn't okay though. None of it was okay.

Lamar's head nodded so low it fell right down onto the table. And when he lifted it back up it was as though he'd just woken. Oh shit, oh shit, he was saying. 'I never could read lips,' Oskar said. 'But I could read those ones.'

By now Eva's voice had risen to a shout.

'This was *your* idea, Lamar. That boat, that car, that fucking lighthouse – it was *yours*.'

'Oh shit, oh shit,' said Lamar.

And then Eva's voice had gone somewhere that was beyond even shouting.

'I went there and I couldn't find them, Lamar. I went there and

I couldn't fucking find them. I went there and I couldn't...'

And then she was running away, along the road at first and then onto the tracks.

Lamar got up and went into the house. When he came out a few moments later he followed the direction Eva had taken, until he reached the tracks. He checked in both directions and, when he was sure he couldn't see her, he walked back and sat at the table. He'd sat there for a while before he suddenly jumped up and flung it over onto the grass. He kicked it. He stomped on it. He snapped off three of its legs. Then he went back into the house. The next time Oskar saw him coming out the door he was carrying a can of gas.

'Which way did she run?' I asked.

'She ran to my place.'

I looked down the tracks.

'How do you know?'

'Know what?'

'That she went to your place.'

'Oh, I know,' he said. 'I know because she stole my boat.'

Into The Wind

Oskar and I got up to go fetch the canoe from behind our shed.

'You should wait for your dad to get back,' he said, kicking an iron ore pellet across the tracks like a shy child. Behind us the pillars of smoke from Butterfly Creek were dispersing into a yellow-brown haze.

'I can't,' I said.

'That's fair enough,' he said.

'It was me who showed her where it was.'

'I guess so.'

We carried the canoe down to the water.

'Can we set out now,' I asked.

'Okay,' he said. He took off his baseball cap and ran the back of his hand over his black eyebrows and forehead. He was sweating. The paddle was shaking in his hand.

All morning there'd been no wind. The moment we got into the canoe one picked up from the north and started blowing into our faces. There was a joke around Crooked River about how it was hard to get lost in a canoe because whichever direction you needed to go in, that's where the wind would be coming from. By the time we got close to the two small islands the waves were already beginning to rise. An eagle stood on one of the islands and watched us approach. He was a familiar fixture; we often left our fish guts out there for him. He eyed us reproachfully as we passed slowly by without stopping.

We passed everything slowly by. For a while it seemed like each of the three bigger islands was paddling along with us, it took us so long to get past them. Out on the main body of the lake the waves had risen higher and some were tipped with white. The undulations of the northern shoreline appeared as fixed and out-of-reach as Tantalus's supper while we tilted up and down from crest to trough like children on a see-saw, Oskar sweating in the stern, me heaving and flailing in the bow. It took us a long time to reach the leech pond.

There, cocooned in the bush, the water was almost still. The gusts that found their way through the trunks and branches riffled it here and there, as though an invisible hand were caressing an animal's fur. We pulled up quietly on the shore to rest.

Oskar sat down beside the remains of the fire we'd built to dry me out after I'd fallen in because of the beaver's tail. The coals and ash looked as historical as the coals and ash in the barrel stove at the prison site. Above them, Oskar's face seemed like it had been seeped in a wash of their reflected shades and colours. Around the darkness of his hair his skin appeared grey and tired. And for the first time I really saw him as old and knew he was old and had a true intimation of what old really was. His chest was heaving thinly beneath the flannel of his shirt and it took him a while before he could get his breath to speak.

'You know,' he said, 'maybe you'd best take this next bit on your own. I'm all out of puff. You can pick me up on the way back.'

'Sure,' I said. I wanted to say I was sorry I'd made him come this far.

We both looked down into the ash of the old fire. The wind

flickered through the tops of the trees; somewhere over by the prison a hawk tipped its wings into an up-draught and rose high above them. It called once and then glided silently away. This could be a lonely place.

'You'll find her,' Oskar said. 'You'll find her just fine.'

'I hope so,' I said.

I'd got back up and grabbed hold of my paddle and was just about to leave when he spoke again. He didn't lift his eyes from the ash of the fire.

'Maybe it's better this way,' he said. I didn't say anything. He took off his hat and ran his hand through his hair.

'I've not been so lucky,' he said sadly. 'It seems like I always ended up finding dead people.'

Second Skins

Oskar's boat was where we'd left it before, where the creek petered out. By the time I set out through the bush the sun was high in the south and the wind had switched to the west. Within the cover of the trees you could barely feel either of them.

The summer forest is the hardest to find your way in, the hardest to see in. When I was a child my mother had occasionally taken me with her when she went to search for shed antlers. She never looked for them in the summer. She'd wait until all the leaves had fallen or else until the snow had melted and they hadn't yet come out. The difference between August and late October or May was the difference between a window with the blinds open and one with them shut.

I remember how intently she searched and how confidently she moved, as if she was seeing and marking everything in the forest at once and didn't ever doubt the direction in which her strides were taking her. She knew the bush. She knew it better than almost anybody. And I could feel that knowledge. In that grey-green place, breathing in the mineral damp of moss and the strange sweetness of the dead leaves, I had felt it. If she got too far ahead of me I'd search through the trees for the colour of her hair, as if it were a will-o-the-wisp leading me towards a place where I could never be lost.

I was useless at finding anything. Keep an eye out for stuff that looks like bone, my mother had told me. And I had. I'd looked and looked until it was as if the pale trunks and branches of the birch and poplar trees were all bone, as though the forest were the remains of an enormous and long-dead animal and we were wandering through its bare and endless ribs.

Once, by chance, I'd discovered the skin of a garter snake. It was so fragile and translucent that at first it felt as though I'd discovered some wondrous and airy jewel, and then my mother had told me what it was and I'd let it fall to the ground and begun blubbering and wailing.

'What's the matter?' she'd asked.

'It lost its skin,' I'd wailed. I'd pictured a terrible nakedness; a fleshy red tube writhing on the earth.

'But there's another one beneath,' she'd said, gently brushing my hot cheek with her cool fingers. 'It grows a new one before it gets rid of its old one.'

'Do you promise?'

'I promise?'

This time I travelled recklessly and impatiently, thinking of bones and skin and things that had been cast away. I crashed through branches and stumbled over windfall, paying no attention, leaving no signs. I was like a panicked animal, an explorer gone berserk. I was surprised when the trees began to thin in front of me and I caught the tell-tale flash of light on water. It was Hummingbird Lake. I was surprised again when I got closer to the shoreline and discovered Eva sitting out on the small island.

The first thing I noticed was her hair. It was her real hair, and appeared to be cropped even shorter than when I'd seen it before. Here and there I could see patches of the same rubbed, raw skin as there was on her neck. I was standing amongst some cedars and (whether it was because of them or not, I didn't know) she didn't seem able to see me. While I was watching she stood up and walked slowly to the water's edge, paused for a second, and then began to wade in. She was wearing an incredibly old-fashioned style of dress, almost an historical one; it had two big pockets at the front and looked like something the old woman who lived in the shoe might have worn, or the ladies who'd taught a young Mrs Schneider to make homesteaders.

She walked in all the way to her waist and then paused again. Her eyes were fixed on a point above me and the trees. There was something oddly relaxed in her expression, languid even. It reminded me of an illustration I'd seen of an opium den in one of the ancient western novels we'd inherited from my grandfather. The dress, which I'd expected to balloon up to the surface, stayed completely under the water.

She began moving again, until the water was almost up to her shoulders, and then paused once more. She tilted her head sideways, to the left, as if she might any second rest her head on the surface of the lake, as though it was a pillow. There was a longer pause this time. I could see a raven circling above the island but couldn't hear its wings; close to my foot the throat of a green frog was mutely swelling and shrinking. Nothing was making a sound. And then Eva turned suddenly around, walked back to the island, and sat down. After ten or so minutes she got back up and did the exact same thing.

All the while I remained as still as a heron on the shore. I couldn't move or speak or cry out. Everything was quiet. I was caught in a kind of paralysis; it was like what happened to me near the swamp house, when everything went silent, except this time it was in my limbs as well as my ears and tongue. And perhaps the worst of it was the stunned and almost lethargic acceptance. Part of me wanted to stay absolutely still while the world skipped forward – perversely welcoming the relief of everything, however bad, having at least happened.

There wasn't a third time. Maybe there wouldn't have been one in any case, I don't know, I only know that before there could be I was wading into the lake. A few feet out the bottom dropped right off and I had to swim. I didn't think once of what was below me.

As I heaved myself onto the shore of the island Eva didn't stand up, or even properly acknowledge I was there. She had that look in her eyes as if she was drunk. Twice she tried to say something and her lips twitched open and closed like a sea creature trying to catch something in the current. If she'd managed to speak she would have slurred. Gently, without saying a word, I reached over and took two stones out of the pockets of her dress. They were heavy and wet. Then I sat down beside her.

On the shore opposite us a squirrel was ferrying a pinecone between two rocks. It kept hiding it behind one rock and then scurrying back, grabbing it, and hiding it behind the other one.

'Jesus H Christ, squirrel – make up your frigging mind!' Eva said.

She reached out and grabbed something from behind a log. A cloud of green death bulged out into the air and stung my eyes. Her eyes had cleared.

'Well,' she said after a few moments, 'that could've gone much better.'

'I guess so,' I said.

'How'd you know I'd be here?'

'I just did.'

She stubbed her cigarette out into a clump of moss. There

173

were bug bites all over her hands. They were all over her neck and face too.

'What happened after I left?' she said. 'Was Lamar looking for me?'

'Lamar burnt the boat.'

'Jesus.'

'And the lighthouse.'

'Jesus Christ.'

'And the Oldsmobile.'

'Jesus H Christ.'

I didn't mention the cabin.

Eva lit a second green death and looked out across the lake. The sun was high in the south and the water was spangled with light. The bugs skittering across its surface winked in and out of view. Sometimes it was hard to tell if they were moving on water or on light.

'I don't know if I could,' she said.

I didn't ask what it was she didn't know.

'Part of me thinks this should have been the place. Part of me is always going to think that. Does that make sense?'

'I guess so,' I said, even though I wasn't sure it did. I wasn't sure if I really understood any of this. But that was okay. There were shapes and pieces. And that would have to be enough.

'We should get going,' I said.

After Eva had finished her second cigarette she went around to the other side of the island and began wading into the lake. A few feet in she turned back to me.

'If you go this way it never gets deeper than your knees,' she said.

174

Green Thoughts In Green Shades

In the bush it's not when everything appears unfamiliar that you have to worry: you know you're lost when everything looks the same.

I'd seen the same tree about ten times and passed over the same ridge as many. Each patch of bog and clump of cattails seemed familiar. If mosquitoes had individual voices then I was getting to know each one of them. I stopped beside the uplifted roots of a fallen tree. 'I think we're lost,' I said. It was late in the afternoon and I was tired and hungry. We'd been walking for hours.

'No kidding,' Eva said. 'What happened to all your broken branches and signs?'

'I can't see them.'

'They're not much good if you can't see them. It's just a waste of a branch.'

'I know.'

'The tree might've needed that branch. What about moss and stuff? You can get your direction from that, can't you?'

'Not really.' There was moss everywhere on the forest floor, in every direction. Eva seemed happy to be lost. Ever since we'd left the lake she'd seemed happy.

'Why Zachary Taylor,' she crooned in her southern accent, 'I suppose we'll have to wait for the stars to guide us.'

'Please,' I said. 'Can you please shut up!'

'My, my, who's got ants in their pants. You should consider yourself lucky: I think I've got every other frigging bug in mine.'

'Please,' I said.

Eva sat down on the moss and leaned back against the roots of the fallen tree. 'Fine. You navigate away there, Mr Pathfinder,' she said. 'I'm having a rest.'

I kept searching for landmarks but when everything begins to look the same nothing is an anything-mark. I felt like one of my father's explorers. The exhilaration of lostness had become the pure animal panic of it. Part of me wanted to run wildly through the bush and not stop until my legs gave out. I would wander through it endlessly, desperate and ragged and windigo-eyed.

'This is how it usually goes in my father's notebooks,' I thought, and then realised I'd said.

'What books?'

'Nothing,' I said. 'It's nothing.'

'You know, Zachary, there's really only one question you have to ask yourself in this position.'

'What's that?' I asked, a bit dizzy and tight-chested.

'What would Gunther have done?'

'But Gunther–' I began and then kept my mouth shut. Slowly, my panic began to subside and my closed mouth became a smile. 'What would he have done?' I asked.

I ended up sitting on the moss beside her. We sat there for what seemed like a long time. Sometimes we spoke, sometimes we didn't. At one point I remember a woodpecker – one of the big, pileated ones – landed on the fallen tree. He looked in our direction and, astonished to find us there, screeched and flew away, disappearing through the woods in swift, swooping rises and glides.

'Thank you,' Eva said.

There was still plenty of light left in the day. We'd been sitting for long enough for the rest of the woods to get used to us. The squirrel in the nearby tree had stopped chiding.

Some small brown birds had perched in the branches. A mouse or a vole or a shrew ran past my feet – I couldn't tell which. And I wondered if this summer world was so very different from the world under the snow that Judith had told me about. I wondered if whatever lived in it spent their time there imagining that other, summer world; if they missed it; if the melting away of the snow and the arrival of the full, unobstructed beams of the sun was a revelation to them – the shapes and pieces made whole – or just like the turning of the leaves, simply a sign of the changing seasons. A thing could become another thing but still stay the same. A place could too. It was quiet and I wasn't scared anymore. Sometimes the best thing you can do when you're lost is stay still.

'Why do you like ruins?' I asked Eva.

'I don't know,' she said. And then after a while she said, 'I guess because they show there's always an afterwards.'

It was so quiet and green under the branches of the trees. It was peaceful and calm. It would be okay if we couldn't find our way out. It would be fine if nobody found us.

'What really happened to your mom, Zack?'

'My mother killed herself,' I said. 'And I don't know why.'

The Long Day

'You've been walking in circles.'

My eyes opened onto Oskar's face. He was looking down at me and at first I was most surprised by the angle – since as far back as I could remember we'd either been the same height or I'd been taller.

'I left markers, I left signs,' I croaked. I was embarrassed to be lost in front of him. He didn't look quite so old as he had when I'd left him earlier.

'Not much good if you can't see them.'

'That's what I told him,' Eva chimed in. She was standing behind him. I didn't know how long the pair of them had been watching me while my eyes had been shut.

'You were sleeping,' Eva said.

'I was just resting my eyes.'

'Sure,' she said. 'If resting your eyes is sleeping then that's what you were doing.'

Oskar was silent as we followed him through the bush. When we got to the boat he ushered us into it with his hand. He pulled the engine cord and set off down the creek without a word. I could tell he was pleased.

'Why's he not speaking?' Eva asked me over the splutter of the engine.

'It's a Finnish thing,' I said.

'Of course,' she said.

On our way back Eva reached over and dipped her fingers

into the surface of the water. They left a tiny rooster tail of spray in their wake, which flew backwards and splashed into my face. It was cool and soft like a mist or drizzle. The sun was just beginning to edge down towards the horizon. We were close to an equinox. It felt like we were in a day that wouldn't end.

As we rounded the first of the bigger islands and came in sight of the bay, Eva pulled her hand out of the water and took hold of mine. Her skin felt cold and clean, as if it had come up from the very bottom of the lake, from deep beyond the drop-off.

'We don't get to,' she shouted at me over the noise of the engine.

'Get to what?'

'We don't get to know why.'

I could see the full curve of the bay and the rocky line of the headland and the grey bulk of the Toad. I could see our dock and my father and Judith standing on it. I could see all of it.

'And that's okay,' Eva shouted. 'It's okay.'

My father's face was taut and pale, as though the sun of the long day hadn't touched it. He reached down from the dock and offered me his hand. His arm looked like a piece of sailor's rope, stringy and sinewy as though twined with hemp. His hand smelt like dish soap and polish. It wouldn't let go of mine, even when I was safely on the dock.

'I brought you out a sweater,' he said.

'Thanks,' I said. It was still twenty something degrees out. Judith said what he must have been thinking.

'Where were you?' she said. 'We were so worried.'

'They got lost,' Oskar said, not moving out of the boat. 'But they're here now.' Eva was already up on the dock.

'Your uncle's been looking everywhere,' Judith said to her. 'He's been frantic.'

'He's in the Burn,' my father said. 'The old Burn,' he quickly added.

'Can I take her there?' I asked.

'Sure,' he said. He still hadn't let go of my hand.

As we were passing the cabin I stopped.

'Wait here,' I said and ran into it.

In my bedroom I pushed everything off my dresser and opened it. The blanket was still wrapped around my mother's sculptures. I peeled it away and looked at them. And then I grabbed the blanket and ran back out.

'Here,' I said, handing it to Eva. 'I found this in the water. It's got a sunrise on it – or a sunset. I'm not sure which.'

'Where did you find it?'

'Under the water,' I said. 'It doesn't matter where.'

'Take it,' I said. 'It's something for you.'

Eva and I walked up the tracks towards the Burn. Beyond it you could still see thin lines of smoke rising up over Butterfly Creek.

'He really burnt it?' said Eva.

'He really did,' I said.

'All of it?'

'All of it.'

'The crazy bastard,' she said and smiled.

Before we reached the Burn I looked back towards the bay. There wasn't anyone on our dock anymore. Oskar had already taken off in his boat. I watched him round the Toad and disappear.

We walked through the black square where Mrs Molson's house had been, our shoes crunching over the charcoaled floor. Fireweed was sprouting through it. At the edge, where the back steps had been, the grass was returning. The smell of smoke from Lamar's place was in the air and for a second I had a premonition – or not a premonition, not exactly, but a strong and sudden sense of afterwards; it was as if we were passing through what Lamar's place would be one day; as though we were already in the future, walking through its ruins. Eva lit a green death and felt her blanket and we made our way along the finger of the Burn.

Lamar was sitting on the boulder by the creek, below the blackened domes of the hills. He was staring into it. Without saying anything, Eva made her way down towards him and I stayed where I was. As she approached closer he lifted his head and was about to stand but I could see her gesture to him and so he stayed sitting. When she got there she sat beside him.

And that's where I left them. On the far bank of the creek I noticed the air was still and empty. The hummingbirds had gone.

I'd meant to go straight back home to the cabin but when I came to the tracks I paused there for a while. I closed my eyes and then opened them quickly. The sun was getting low in the west and the surface of the bay was alive with its glittering light. And I remembered the train depositing the three of us at the lake and us standing here watching the caboose disappear around the bend and then that first turning of our heads to glimpse the lake's waters. The light on that water – that was what I thought about then. And I think of it still. And if I have ever seen some small portion of eternity it was there and is there and will always be there.

Acknowledgements

I have incurred many debts in arriving at the point where *Hummingbird* could take flight. The research and writing of this novel was made possible with the support of an AHRC fellowship in the creative and performing arts. I would also like to thank my colleagues at Cardiff, Richard Gwyn, Shelagh Weekes, and Tim Rhys, for their friendship and many wise words about the art, and occasional travails, of writing. For helping to bring this book into the world I'd like to thank Richard and everyone at Parthian Books, as well as Veronique Baxter at David Higham Associates.

None of my books would ever have been possible without the love and support of the Hughes clan in Wales - and this book is no different. I am also incredibly thankful to the Fotheringham clan in Canada, and to James Burns for showing me the wilderness ropes and where the geese hide.

And finally, I owe a huge debt of gratitude to Lisa Solomon (and Lenny) for making a wonderful and happy home for this book out at Eva Lake. It would not have been written without it. There were times afterwards when I doubted *Hummingbird* would find its wings and for restoring my confidence, and making me see it all as an adventure again, I am deeply grateful to Lisa Lucas for her generous, astute and unfailing encouragement. In both cases, I have been more fortunate than I could have ever hoped and am more thankful than I could ever express. Diolch o galon.